A HOUSE IN VIENNA

A HOUSE IN VIENNA

BY MARIANNE PHILIPS

TRANSLATED FROM THE DUTCH BY
IRENE CLEPHANE & DAVID HALLETT

HARCOURT, BRACE AND COMPANY

NEW YORK

Published in Holland as "Bruiloft in Europa"

839.31
P554bE

COPYRIGHT, 1936, BY

HARCOURT, BRACE AND COMPANY, INC.

first American edition

Designed by Robert Josephy

PRINTED IN THE UNITED STATES OF AMERICA
BY QUINN & BODEN COMPANY, INC., RAHWAY, N. J.

A HOUSE IN VIENNA

THE house stood in the Luftbadgasse. It had stood there for two hundred years, and of that time it had belonged to the Hodl family a good hundred. They had come originally from Tyrol, but for more than a century they had been settled in Vienna, a fruitful, industrious family of master painters. For the golden wedding of Johannes Hodl and Resi, his wife, all their children, grandchildren, and great-grandchildren were to be photographed together, and from the picture pages of the daily papers the whole of Vienna would be able to judge how very fruitful and how very industrious this family must be to have produced and reared so many descendants. It was not the ordinary golden wedding of an old couple celebrating their last ceremonial feast-day on earth. No, it was the manifestation of its mysterious vitality by a still firmly rooted bit of old Vienna; and the parish priest of Mariahilf would bestow his blessing upon it when the Hodls attended high Mass at eleven o'clock. Already, at six o'clock in the morning, neighbors and apprentices were busy adorning the house in honor of the occasion.

The main entrance hall was as large as a ballroom —and that day was to serve as one. It was paved with colored antique floor tiles that had withstood undamaged the ravages of time and traffic: the hall had been cleared, and their complicated baroque pattern came as a surprise.

On the right of the entrance hall lay Hodl's home. It was smaller than the flats upstairs that were let, and when the Hodl family was at its maximum must have been considerably overpopulated. To the left lay the workshop, from which overflowed into the hall innumerable superfluities such as drying cupboards and billboards, ladders, carts and so on. But today, of course, these had been removed.

Actually, the spacious entrance hall had formerly been merely a passage leading to the yard at the back upon which the upper flats looked out; but long ago a fourth wall had been added to the entrance hall, shutting it off from the yard, and now only a little doorway in this wall gave access to the wilderness that lay behind Hodl's house. But that little doorway was still in regular use, for in the yard stood a curious little pavilion put up for some unknown purpose by the first owner, before the house belonged to a Hodl: but a certain indecorous intention was revealed in its gallant wall paintings. It was let for a song, because it could be reached only through the turpentiny atmosphere of the workshop or across the wilderness of the neglected backyard. It seemed predestined to serve as a refuge for Bohemians, and had in fact been that so long as anyone could remember. At the mo-

4

ment, a still undiscovered genius of a violinist nursed four cats and a chronic melancholia there.

The little pavilion never received a ray of sunshine; but in this respect it was not less favored than the large house against which it leaned, for that in its turn lay in the shadow cast by the backs of the houses on Gumpendorferstrasse. The Luftbadgasse lay completely in their shadow—the deep shadow of a back street where the houses are not kept up because the sunlight never shines on them to show up their lack of paint. But Hodl, of course, was bound by his trade to keep his façade in order, and in consequence he undoubtedly possessed the most considerable house in the street. Still, that entailed no great effort, for the Luftbadgasse, which lay some five yards below the level of the Gumpendorferstrasse and could be entered only at one end, because the other entrance by the Apollo Theatre was cut off by a *Stieg* of four-and-thirty steps, was by its situation destined to be a stillborn street in which an architect had seldom built a house with noticeable pleasure. Only such people as were not particular about their address or had withdrawn themselves from life cared to live there.

The ground floors were occupied by small tradesmen: good, old-fashioned master tailors who knew how to cut a respectable bob-tailed coat better than a "smoking" and therefore had little to do; several custom shoemakers who had nothing to do at all.

5

A furrier, once head of a workshop that supplied the court, removed the worst blemishes from rabbit skins bought in the Naschmarkt and made them up into linings for cheap coats for the department stores. There was also the man who made plaster models, but who draws from plaster-of-Paris nowadays? Only the little coal-and-wood shop flourished in this damp neighborhood; but of course it did not improve the general aspect of the street, and was a thorn in the flesh of Hodl the landlord. But was it reasonable to expect the municipal street cleaner to sweep the pavements regularly in a little street where his truck could not even turn round?

So much for the ground floors, but the dwellings above them concealed little that invited greater rejoicing. The Luftbadgasse (where perhaps an open-air bath had once been projected, but which, in fact, offered scant fresh air and no bathing facilities in any of the houses) had become, chiefly through its situation, a refuge for the human derelicts of the imperial epoch. It was but a quarter of an hour's walk from the Ring, the Hofburg, the Kärntnerstrasse, and the Opera, a half an hour from Parliament and the Academy. Without paying tram fares, those superfluous officers, head waiters, piano teachers, architects, civil servants who had been swept down in one avalanche with the Emperor and the Archdukes until they landed in the depths of the Luftbadgasse could still go and breathe the air of the Innerestadt, take

6

their little daily walk along the Ring, or sit in the Kaisergarten—which none of them was prepared to call the Burggarten in accordance with the new name-plates. When they left their flats, although they walked on worn-out heels, it was very correctly and with an elastic gait. They sported a monocle or an artist's slouch hat with outmoded elegance, and did not know that they stood out among the tweed suits and trench coats of the newer times like figures from a past gone for good. Why, no, they did not fancy themselves at all. For the moment, of course, they were not on the winning side. But patience: times were changing. Soon they would be implored to come back.

And then of course there was the usual floating population of every cheap quarter in a capital. Several ballet girls from the Opera who had recently had to accept a further reduction of salary lived there; several clerks with their families; and at the back of the houses, many, many unemployed with little children who were not allowed to play with the other children because their fathers belonged to the tidy unemployed who every morning went out to try their luck with some ridiculous merchandise in a despatch case. No, the Luftbadgasse was far from being a working-class district.

Johannes Hodl had fortunately let his house very nicely. When during an occasional wakeful hour at night he reviewed in his mind the human contents of his premises, he felt himself privileged above other house-owners. On the first floor left (with the bay window) lived Herr Friedemann. During the war he had manufactured spaghetti and macaroni from ground straw and potato flour, but he had lost his happily acquired wealth through peace and inflation. He now lent small sums to the petty bourgeoisie at a high rate of interest and still earned much more than enough for his own not innocent hobbies, besides the little it took to feed his fat poodle and an old second cousin who kept house for him. On his right, in four dark rooms, Kerner, the pensioned Counselor of Justice, had housed the remains of his collection of antique furniture. It would last his time: he had just been living for three months off a writing-desk, and possessed a unique and beautiful table inlaid with mosaic that would certainly keep him alive for two years, him and his old paralyzed wife.

On the second floor left with the bay window lived Maria Ritter, once a world-famous coloratura singer. In 1916 she had been pensioned by the management of the Opera and, strange to relate, her pension had since then been only slightly reduced; but then, Vienna is after all the city of music. The flat on the right housed Herr Bergmann with his wife and five little daughters under ten. Of him there was nothing to be said except that he was the husband of Hodl's youngest daughter, and that he would certainly remain for life head clerk of his small insurance office, unless indeed it failed prematurely. He had been al-

lowed to let his front room to Fräulein Goldös, the
pretty head-cashier at Korngross's, and about her a
great deal might be said, but little that was unpleasant.

On the third floor, on the expensive, though not
really too expensive, side (there was no bay window
here), lived Meyer Jonathan, and it was absolutely
inexplicable how he had got into the Luftbadgasse,
for he belonged—there was no gainsaying it—to the
neighborhood of the Hohe Markt or to the Leo-
poldstadt: he was scribe to the Jewish congregation;
but there must always be exceptions, and Meyer
Jonathan was indeed an exceptional man. Hodl had
to admit it. So long as Meyer's grandson, who lived
with him, did not preach subversive doctrines to the
apprentices, Hodl would not begrudge the old Jew a
place under his roof. In the circumstances, however,
he felt that the flat on the third floor left was not quite
satisfactorily let.

On the other hand, the small flat on the third floor
right gave him abundant cause for satisfaction. There
lived an aging needlework teacher with her mother,
and although he had let them the cheapest little flat,
right under the roof, at a truly insignificant rent,
Hodl bowed with the most profound politeness when
they passed him in the entrance hall, for the old lady
was an authentic countess. When he carried the dust-
bin upstairs for her daughter, he would not hear of
thanks: "Don't mention it, countess." Her small name-

9

plate by the great main gate was a daily pleasure to him. Von Wernizek-Bolnanyi: all Vienna knew the name and family, even though it was ruined and had been deprived of nobility since '18. Yes, No. 12 Luftbadgasse was certainly the most important house in the street.

Architecturally it was not to be underrated either. It was real old Viennese baroque, although no one had ever apprised Hodl of the fact, and he was simply rather in love with his agreeable, solid, two-hundred-year-old premises. Only the sandstone figures along the cornice pleased him but moderately. They had originated in the love of ornamentation of the second Hodl, who in 1874 had added the medallions with Haydn, Beethoven, and Mozart: at that period there was much building and decorating everywhere in Vienna, and besides being a master painter he had also been the trombone player of his musical society. Johannes Hodl, who had been married just fifty years, could still remember how the house looked in his youth before the sandstone figures were added. If he were to follow his inclination, they would be removed that very day, but in his seventy-second year he still retained a little piety and respect for his father. His children could do what they thought fit about them.

Neighbors and workmen were busy decorating the whole house-front with greenery, and they had taken the opportunity to give a jollier appearance to the old gentlemen on the cornice, who were now wearing, the three of them, crowns of fir green. Beethoven looked disconsolate under his, but Mozart wore his with a sprightly air, and good papa Haydn had been provided by an apprentice with an extra bunch of greenery in the bow of his pigtail. Small boys and ample matrons from adjacent ground-floor dwellings gave instructions from below concerning the hanging of the paper chains and garlands along the windows of the first and second floors. They stood nodding approval as they watched the foreman fix in the center above the main gate a heart-shaped, shining gilt shield upon which was scrolled in hard blue the letters and figures *Heil dem Goldnen Paar, 1883-1933.*

All these preparations were going on as quietly and carefully as possible, and at a very early hour, because they were of course to be a surprise for the pair whose golden wedding it was. Johannes Hodl at least had done no more than turn round once in his bed when he heard the hammer blows: he was a kind-hearted man, and did not grudge anybody a bit of fun—nor himself either.

But Mother Resi beside him found it very difficult not to put her feet out of bed. True, the night before her eldest daughter had come to say that she was to do nothing, absolutely nothing on her feast-day, and that little Resi and Maria would arrive at half-past six in order to start the whole business; but she knew very well how things went when such matters were

11

left to young girls. Besides which, it was of course quite impossible for anyone else to put out the linen from the large mahogany press of which she alone had a key. Even at her many confinements, everything needed, and more, had always been laid ready in a drawer of the chiffonier. But how could she put out the table linen when the children would not tell her who had been invited and who had not? No, Resi lay not without worry in her fifty-year-old marriage bed, and now that worry was upon her, even on this day, it attacked her from many different points.

"Did you manage to put everything away in the workshop?" she asked Hodl. She meant: Had the entrance hall been completely cleared, and could it later on be thoroughly scrubbed into a proper dance floor? But a woman never says exactly what she thinks. Johannes Hodl grunted, "Yes," and turned on his other side. He was not sleeping, and did not want to sleep either, for he was sufficiently rested, but he was lying comfortably and lazily enjoying his good feather bed, from which today he need not rise early in order to see if his workmen were arriving on time.

Resi also turned on her other side. She could not lie still, for she was not by any means sure that the entrance hall had been cleared. And then suddenly she could hold out no longer. She threw back the cover from her thin, blue-veined, old woman's legs and sat on the side of the bedstead.

But Johannes could not permit that. What would

the children and the neighbors say if Mother did not allow herself to be surprised? "Woman," he cried, "will you find no rest until you're in your coffin?" Seizing her with his still strong worker's hands he pulled her back onto the pillows and then, because it was the anniversary of his wedding and because he still had good memories of his first wedding day, he drew her closer to him, pressed her small gray head to his shoulder, and said: "Be still, now, you little fusser." Yes, and he had also said something like that on his first wedding day. They both had to smile, and Resi lay still again for quite ten minutes, her small birdlike head pressed close against Hodl's familiar, breathing breast.

But then the clock in the sitting-room struck half-past six. Maria and little Resi arrived, admitted noiselessly by the foreman, but Mother still had that sharp hearing of hers, and now there was no holding her back. She must be present at the preparations in her living-room. At a master painter's, trestles and boards were to be had for the asking, and the horseshoe-shaped table had already been set up. The furniture had disappeared under greenery, and someone had brought a gramophone. Resi took in everything at a glance when she put her head round the door, but she was received with cries of "Don't come in!"

Yes: but who could prevent a still active housewife, the mother of a hundred descendants, from doing anything she had got it into her head to do? And so, imperturbably, Resi ran into her own living-room, and nobody dared prevent her. She gave her orders, distributed tablecloths and napkins, climbed onto a chair to the topmost shelf of her sideboard in front of the largest cut-glass bowl, and with an expert tongue tasted to see if the *Hirschhörnchen*, which her second daughter had baked by the hundred these last days, would do honor to her and to her house.

The *Hirschhörnchen* were perfect, but as she was considering them between the tip of her tongue and her palate, to decide whether yeast or at any rate baking powder had been worked into the paste, fear seized her in the legs: she had forgotten she ought to have remained fasting until the hour of communion, and now, confused and distressed, she ran back towards the bedroom and Hodl, in order to seek comfort from him as she had done in all the confusing moments of her life.

And then Maria turned the key in the lock of the bedroom door behind her grandmother. Hodl could not help laughing; it was so pleasant just for one whole day to let others do for you anything they wanted. With his friendly heart, he really loved the world and its denizens a great deal. Throughout his life, he had never met anybody who had willingly and knowingly tried to do him harm. Such happy souls do indeed exist. . . .

AT exactly the same time, an old Mercedes stopped on the sandpath along the extreme southern border of the former royal and imperial Laxenburger Schlosspark, some thirteen miles outside Vienna. A young man sprang out and looked about him. Nothing stirred on the green expanse that stretched for miles as far as Mödling. Nothing stirred under the thick oak trees of the park, which had been allowed to go wild since 1918. Then he ran up to a little pavilion covered with dashing baroque ornaments, from which, however, the pink stucco was breaking off leprously. He slipped his hand through a small broken window and, when the catch gave, climbed inside. He beckoned, and the second door of the car flew open. Four, five young men sprang over each other out of the car. Then two parcels the length of a man's stature and wrapped in canvas were pushed out of the car door. The door of the pavilion opened from the inside. With a swing, the young men loaded the parcels onto their shoulders and carried them inside. Nobody had said a word.

Five minutes later the Mercedes was proceeding calmly at a leisurely pace along the Laxenburger-strasse in the direction of Vienna. The driver of a fuel-truck who gave them the right-of-way saw through the little panes four very ordinary young men. Someone was giving the man behind the wheel a light. Someone at the back was reading a paper, and yawning immeasurably.

OLD Meyer Jonathan had undone his phylacteries and kissed them with concentrated fervor before putting them away in their little silk brocade bag. The bitter, fragrant taste of the leather was still upon his lips, and he smiled as he carefully laid in its folds his tallith, the beautiful white woolen prayer scarf with the black stripes. He ran his fingers once more over the soft fringe, and murmured for the last time: "Blessed art Thou, O Lord our God, who hast hallowed us with Thy commandments!" Then he put away the scarf folded in four in the tallith bag, and with quiet hands opened a drawer and put everything into it.

Nothing stirred as yet in the house about him. The familiar ticking of the clock was like a pulse through the room. On the roof above his head pigeons pattered, and somewhere below a hammer thudded dimly; but these sounds belonged to the stillness. The muslin curtain flapped backwards and forwards in front of the open window as if moved by peaceful breathing, and balmy little gusts of air came to him like a benediction. Meyer Jonathan remained standing in the stillness of God.

Yes, even after a night of care and longing, the

17

morning prayer had brought him back into the stillness of the presence of God.

Many such still moments had Meyer Jonathan lived
in the course of the days. Always of course at morning, noon, and evening prayer. But also when, out of
the bustle of the Innerestadt, he entered his synagogue in the Seitenstettengasse, at peace like a field
laborer who, wending home his weary way, lifts the
latch of his door. The walls of the synagogue that
enclosed him were like protecting walls around his
soul. But the stillness was only complete when, at
home in his own room in the evening under the lamp,
with his quill pen he placed the Hebrew signs on the
stiff, living parchment, the beloved letters which,
each in itself small and inconsiderable, together constituted the Word. Sheet after sheet and scroll after
scroll he had thus filled during his life, and always
as he went along he had murmured the words that
grew under his hand. Many, many texts and proverbs,
Scrolls of the Law and Mezuzahs, a whole life long,
and ever and again as a refrain came therein the
glad tidings, "Hear, O Israel! the Lord thy God, the
Lord is one!"

It was the deepest certainty of the Doctrine, and
when he uttered it, the smile in Meyer Jonathan rose
up towards the bright stillness of God.

Meyer Jonathan was eighty. His hair and his beard
were silver-white, but behind his spectacles his eyes
grew younger from year to year. Whoever spoke to

him and looked at him felt his attention suddenly riveted, wanted to sink into Meyer's eyes and find rest there, as a man seems to become one with the smile of an innocent child. But Meyer Jonathan had more than a youthful ingenuousness in his clear eyes. There was something else there too, something for which people have no name since it lies beyond the pale within which human understanding allots names. The gaze of those who spoke with him was held in a longing to get nearer to this mysterious thing he was aware of, this nameless clarity; and then Meyer Jonathan would smile and take off his steel spectacles and become again a little white-haired Jew with a hundred tiny delicate wrinkles round his large nose and a slight panting cough. Thus he went among the people, and nobody need see that God walked with him.

Meyer had made his bed, and the bread left over from his breakfast he had scattered on the window-sill for the pigeons. Many people in the Luftbadgasse did that. Pigeons roosted under every neglected roof, in every unused hiding-place. Everywhere in old Vienna pigeons roost; but not in the large, newly built blocks of flats that the Vienna municipality has squeezed in among the old slums. In the Luftbadgasse hundreds of pigeons went pattering along the façades and the pavement. They cooed and made love and flapped their wings on high as they emerged from corners in the roofs. Playfully they planed high up in the air, and below they found food spread ready on the windowsills. But nobody fed them with such regularity and devotion as Meyer Jonathan. The pretty, reddish-blonde lady who nodded to him so pleasantly from one of the back windows of the Gumpendorferstrasse also looked after the pigeons well, and certainly with a more lavish hand, but she sometimes let several days go by. Meyer Jonathan never did.

This time the pigeons had received the greater part of his breakfast. He himself ate only a single sliver of bread. How could an old man who had lain waiting anxiously hour after hour for a footstep feel hunger? But pray the morning prayer, make the bed, and breakfast, all that he was required to do, even though he had spent a night of anxiety over the son of his son. The God of Israel does not expect His people to be superhuman, but He expects trust in the life that has once been received from Him, and attention to every human need. Consequently, Meyer Jonathan after he had breakfasted looked out for the dirty linen, his own and that of his grandson Daniel. The charwoman would find it later on in a corner of the little kitchen. But as he laid Daniel's blue striped shirt on the top and smoothed it over the pile with careful fingers, his contracted throat swallowed with difficulty the last bit of his breakfast. He suddenly visualized Daniel, his round sturdy neck and arms

20

still damp with cold water, pulling his shirt of a morning over his curly brown head with a jerk, and his heart inquired: 'Daniel, where are you? What are you doing? Who's preparing your morning coffee today?'

Meyer Jonathan had childish notions of student life. He thought that Daniel Jonathan, the law student, could find happiness in study for study's sake, and that he must be at his happiest behind his desk. He thought that in 1933 at the University of Vienna one could turn as resolutely away from the world as he and his friends had done sixty years ago, when they buried themselves in their Talmud researches at the Jewish seminary in Cracow. That was why he was anxious about Daniel, who had apparently felt no longing for his desk for two days and nights. If he had not been so childishly ignorant of the driving, struggling life of his city and the world, if he could have sensed that the impersonal passion which sometimes possesses the noble-minded was now the world over driving young men to glowing action and to strife among themselves, then he would not have been so disappointed and anxious over Daniel's erratic comings and goings. But how could a young and fiery revolutionary socialist make a pious old Jew understand the problems and catastrophes of these times? How could he make a wise man living in the peace of God comprehend the beginnings of what Grossdeutsche and Austromarxist, Schutzbündler and Heimwehr, Sozi and Nazi and Bolshevik wanted? It

21

was impossible. The only thing one could do was love him as though one were still a small child, and accept his warm, trusting love as it was given. This Daniel did; and that was why it was strange indeed that he had left his grandfather two days with no news.

Meyer Jonathan closed the window. It was seven o'clock, and he must go to his work. It was true that he need not be at the secretariat before eight, but a man of eighty cannot walk from the Luftbadgasse to the Seitenstettengasse in less than an hour. He thus spent quite a long time outside the house—every day from seven o'clock in the morning till four o'clock in the afternoon. A long day, in which he registered births and deaths and wrote his documents for the archives of the Jewish congregation. And yet that did not constitute his real day. The real living day greeted him in the afternoons at four o'clock on the threshold of his own living-room, when he had put on his black skull-cap and knew he had a whole evening before him in which he could inscribe the Name on the white parchment.

Outside his closed front door, he laid the key under the mat where the charwoman would find it. Daniel knew the place too. If God willed that Daniel should come home—yes, if it were God's will that Daniel should come home again . . .

Meyer Jonathan's eyes were dull as he bent and pushed the key further under the mat. Certainly it was no sin if an old man carried pain in his heart for the son of his son, even though God filled that heart daily with His glory and mercy. God Himself had given him his human heart. It felt pain as sharply as joy; but it did not rebel against the pain, not that. It was God's will that Daniel should consort with goys and unbelievers. It was also God's will that Daniel had stayed away two nights.

And so Meyer Jonathan stood up again, as upright as he could, and with his stick groped on the badly lit landing for the first step of the stairs. His working day had begun. He would have to be extra quick in order to be in time, but at the secretariat nobody should notice that it had cost him an effort. He was eighty, and a scribe's pension was small, too small to keep a student. He must hold out for another year or so. And why should he not? His own father had lived to be ninety-two.

On the landing of the second floor he raised his large black felt hat from his white head to pretty Fräulein Goldös, who had just closed Bergmann's front door behind her. "You're early too," she said, astonished. "I've never met you before in the mornings."

"Then you're earlier than usual, I think," answered Meyer Jonathan, "for I am late today."

"Yes, I'm early. The weather is too fine. I'm going swimming," said Fräulein Goldös. "I should be irritable all day if I hadn't been in the water." And now Meyer saw also the little canvas case. Fräulein

Goldös was wearing a small red hat on her black curls. She was broad in the shoulders, narrow in the hips, fresh and intelligent, and her frank laugh revealed white teeth and a deep note in her voice. She was head cashier at Korngross's and had no worries. In his thoughts, Meyer gave her his blessing. True, she was not a Jewess, but this vital Hungarian proclaimed the same joy of creation. Friendly and pretty she was, God bless her.

"I saw your grandson yesterday," said Fräulein Goldös as she preceded Meyer Jonathan down the stairs, "in the Kärntnerring with a whole lot of other students. They wanted to reach the Kärntnerstrasse, but it had been lined off. It's said the university has been closed again by the Government. Do you know anything about it . . . ? Why, what's the matter now?"

Meyer Jonathan had stumbled over his stick, and was clinging to the banisters. "You've seen Daniel?"

"Yes. There was another of those disturbances in the Kärntnerstrasse: it must be pleasant too for the shopkeepers there, not to mention the fact that this week the Rotarians are having their congress and might have done a lot of shopping. Something seems to have happened to a Jewish student, some sort of a scandal—oh, I don't know what. All child's play: why don't the boys study? Yes, and now the Government is actually going to close the university again. Of course they're fighting in the street now. But why

24

must that happen just in the Kärntnerstrasse? Was that necessary?"

Fräulein Goldös was a business woman. She had been in business for ten years, since her sixteenth birthday, and the Kärntnerstrasse was near to her heart. These days Vienna had to live on foreigners, hadn't it? And who washed its dirty linen in public, just under their eyes? Mischievous boys!

Fräulein Goldös had worked herself up. She jumped the last steps of the staircase, and, waving her hand, called a "Grüss Gott" up to Meyer Jonathan, who stood riveted where she had left him.

"My God! My Redeemer! My Keeper in trouble!" he implored in the words of the morning prayer that still echoed in him. "My Refuge! My Cup of Salvation! My Rock and my Hope!" He drank from the Cup of Salvation, he leaned his tottering body against the Rock, and then he was able to let go. Once more he felt the step of the stairs under his feet. God willing, not a hair of Daniel's head would be touched, even though he had allowed himself to be involved in disturbances. But why had the boy not returned home these two nights?

Meyer reached the entrance hall at last, and even his careworn eyes took note of the unusual sight of the beamed ceiling decorated with dangling Chinese lanterns and hanging fir green. "What's happening here?" he enquired of the foreman; but then he sud-

25

denly recollected. "Congratulations," he said politely, and pressed the hand of Hodl's eldest son.

"There's to be dancing here tonight," said the foreman. "Won't you come and take a turn, Herr Jonathan?"

But Hodl's eldest knew this was an inappropriate question, and pushed the workman to one side. "This afternoon Father and Mother are holding a reception. Shall we see you?"

Meyer Jonathan nodded once or twice. Certainly the Hodls were very worthy people, and to be able to celebrate a golden wedding was a blessing of God. It was right to congratulate people on a thing like that when one had the opportunity. "With pleasure, Herr Hodl," he said.

He hurried down the Luftbadgasse. He was certainly a quarter of an hour late, but the tram he could not take because of the high steps and the cost. He must step out a little, that was all.

In the Gumpendorferstrasse an ambulance drove past him, and he felt a stab at his heart; but ambulances went driving by so often. All the same, he stood still to look after the vehicle until it had passed the entrance to the Luftbadgasse. Then he hurried further along the Gumpendorferstrasse and the empty Eschenbachstrasse. He wanted to cross the Burgring, but at the corner of the Babenbergerstrasse there seemed to be a disturbance. A crowd of young people had gathered. There were cries and gesticulations, and people came running up from all sides. Meyer Jonathan did not cross over. He hurried along with the others. 'What am I doing now?' he thought, but his old legs seemed to know very well what they were doing; and then when he was close, groups of people heaved to and fro, arms were waved on high, the crowd opened, and somebody was thrown right across the road.

"Sjemang Jisroeil," whispered Meyer Jonathan, and, trembling, seemed to feel the thud with which the young man hit the pavement. His knees shook. He could not go on. An uninterrupted stream of people passed him, on their way to their daily work, avoiding the disturbance because they were in a hurry. But Meyer leaned against a lamp-post. Suddenly he was too old and too tired, almost abandoned by life. And still he must walk for another half-hour, walk quickly, if he was to reach the secretariat in time. If only somebody would take him under the arm and conduct him across the road he would be grateful, although as a rule in his obstinate old man's pride he would accept no help.

Several policemen came up to the disturbance. Suddenly everybody scattered, and the lookers-on dispersed. But nobody admonished Meyer Jonathan to move on. The policemen looked over the head of the little old Jew. Meyer Jonathan waited. He wanted to know something: who were these people who could behave so savagely, so paganly? Two young fellows,

27

obviously students, came right up to him. He saw and knew. He had been waiting for that. They were flushed and panting, and one of them had lost his collar. Yes, that's how Daniel would come home, battered and covered in dust like them. And see, one of the boys was bleeding from the nose. It was well he had seen this. Now he would be able to keep a hold on himself when Daniel came home.

But behind these two came three others, two of them supporting the third who, crippled, was trying to limp along. They beckoned a taxi; but what driver was going to allow his cushions to be ruined by a group of battered, bloodstained students? Meyer Jonathan saw the taxi drive by, and he was indignant in his heart that one man could willingly and knowingly leave others in their dire necessity. But at the same time he saw that Daniel was not there; and then he realized that all the time he had been expecting to see Daniel.

At five minutes to eight Meyer Jonathan turned the corner into the Seitenstettengasse, and there—in front of the doors of the secretariat—was Daniel strolling up and down, Daniel himself washed and brushed, without bloodstains, Daniel with his head erect, his dark hair uncovered as always, Daniel with his very own upright carriage. God be praised, there was Daniel.

Meyer Jonathan uttered a short, dry little gasp, but

then he pressed his lips together. There was no need for the boy to know about his anxiety.

Daniel saw his grandfather and stood still before the steps of the secretariat. The old man crossed hurriedly, not carefully enough, for a taxi-driver looked round at him startled and reproving. But Meyer Jonathan had already laid his hands upon Daniel's arms. Daniel's wide-open eyes looked down into his grandfather's face. Meyer Jonathan's smile shone upwards.

But then Meyer dropped his hands. The smile changed into an anxious question. "Has something happened to you, boy?"

He himself found it queer that he should ask that. Nothing had happened to Daniel; he could see that for himself. The boy had not the least scratch. And yet something had happened. The boy's face was not the face he knew. It was strained and cold and white, and above all old. Suddenly Meyer saw his son, Daniel's father, on his deathbed, when he himself had uttered the prayer for the dying. Daniel's face was fixed as that of one who had just died—and still it tried to smile at Meyer Jonathan.

"What's happened?" repeated the old man, and at the same time he knew that Daniel would tell him nothing.

And so it was. Daniel looked into his grandfather's face for something that he could say, but to those loving, careworn eyes he could speak no untruth, and so he merely went on looking at him; but the

29

smile round his mouth grew more alive, his face relaxed. Meyer Jonathan saw it happen and waited.

"I just wanted to see you, grandfather—and I wanted to let you see that there's no need for you to be anxious. I hadn't the time to come home, and then it occurred to me that I could easily come and wait for you here."

"All right, boy, all right," said Meyer Jonathan. "Where have you been all this time?"

"Oh, with friends," said Daniel. Just words. That was no answer. He knew it well, but there was nothing to be done. Here in the middle of the busy pavement it was enough that his grandfather could see him, and that he saw his grandfather; and then suddenly he became aware again that he could not stay longer, that he was being waited for. He looked round towards the empty waiting Mercedes.

"I say, go in now. It's time." He laid his hands upon Meyer's shoulders. A foolish thought flashed through his mind. He could take the old man with him in the car and drive to Hietzing or to the banks of the Danube. There they could lie together in the shadow of the trees, and he would tell him everything, everything of these last days. Together they would share their sorrow, and their aversion, yes, their aversion for all these things. But there would be a great deal to tell, a great deal to explain. To himself also perhaps, and to this old child—who nevertheless was the only one to whom he would have liked to tell everything.

A foolish thought. Under his hands he felt the narrow bony shoulders of the old man, and once more he looked round at the car—foolishness—foolishness. Grandfather did not even know that he could drive. There was much too much his grandfather did not know.

"Go now, quickly," said Daniel. "We've seen each other at least," and he took his hands from Meyer Jonathan's shoulders.

The bells of St. Ruprecht's had begun to ring. As he walked up the steps, Meyer looked round at his grandson once more. The great revolving door of the secretariat thrust him in. Eight o'clock. He was in time after all.

TWENTY-FIVE past eight. The Ostend
Express slowed down. 'Passau, the frontier,' thought
Otto von Wernizek, and got up. Why, he did not really
know. His luggage would not be examined till he
reached Vienna. So he sat down again.

At that moment Mr. Hunter slid open the door of
the compartment. "Well," said he, "were you able to
sleep?"

"Oh, yes," said Otto. "At Frankfort a fellow came
in who snored, but we got rid of him again at Wurz-
burg. I've slept very well."

Mr. Hunter felt ill used. His flat, fleshy face wore
the bothered expression of a disconsolate baby. This
young man was traveling in an ordinary second-class
carriage and had slept. But he, in his first-class
sleeper, had been unable to withdraw himself from
existence for more than ten minutes or so. That was
very unpleasant. It would probably spoil his first day
in Vienna.

But it was really entirely his own fault. He had
not allowed himself to sleep. He had allowed himself to be reminded at every jolt of the carriage
that he was being dragged over European rails
and switch-points which, like so many other things in

32

Europe, were no longer in quite good condition.

Mr. Hunter was not traveling for his pleasure. Unlike some of his friends, who possessed romantic inclinations or wives, he had never for one moment longed to encounter the Old World: he was completely satisfied with America. But he was vice-president of the Midland Rotary Club, and this with devotion, for he believed in practical work, and in the productiveness of every human deed, and therefore also of his own good deeds. How could he then refuse the honor thrust upon him of representing his club at the International Rotary Congress in Vienna?

Certainly Mr. Hunter was not traveling for his pleasure. He owed it to his club to draw up a businesslike report on old Europe, and business competence demanded the right frame of mind.

So far he had been rather dissatisfied with the facts that had confronted him. In Paris chauffeurs drove much too fiercely. The *chansonniers* wore dirty jackets, and the lavatories of his first-class hotel had inadequate ventilation.

"There lies Passau," said Otto von Wernizek, pointing out of the carriage window.

"Another of those frontier stations?" enquired Mr. Hunter. He felt a grim satisfaction whenever at a frontier station a locomotive of still another nationality was hitched on to the train. Of course the unnecessary delay irritated him, but at the same time he chuckled at the obstinacy with which Europe, while

33

assuming it had the monopoly of wisdom, retained its freakish little frontiers. Every new passport officer he received with an audible sigh, and an eyebrow ironically raised.

Otto von Wernizek had by this time given up replying. He surveyed the Danube and drew comparisons with the Ohio. Then suddenly all comparison fell away. He remembered many sunny days and felt himself slipping into cool clear water. 'Six days all to myself in Vienna,' he thought, and smiled. To speak nothing but German for six days, to talk to people who understood him at the first word. Six days free from America.

"Is the boss awake yet?" asked Mr. Hunter.

Otto von Wernizek had long since grown accustomed to Mr. Haymaker's being his boss, and to the fact that he was so called. Besides, Mr. Haymaker, the director of the Midland Orchestra, was not even an unpleasant boss. He had a free-and-easy way of life, and conducted himself democratically. Of course, he was capable of dismissing even a first violin with a week's notice; but that happened to be the way of the New World, and a boss was a boss. But with Passau in sight, Otto von Wernizek, one-time lieutenant in the guards, all the same felt it strange, and becoming steadily stranger, that Mr. Haymaker should be his boss, and he Mr. Haymaker's secretary.

"I haven't seen Mr. Haymaker yet," said Otto.

A long, wilted steward slunk past the doorway,

34

ringing nonchalantly for breakfast. Mr. Hunter beckoned. The steward stood still and waited.

"Tell him to prepare me a grapefruit, Wernizek."

Otto, who for years had been kept going by the kindness of philanthropy, had throughout the journey willingly taken upon himself the task of translating Mr. Hunter's wishes, but with Passau in sight it became more difficult; after all, he was Haymaker's secretary and not the slave of Haymaker's friends. Nevertheless, he ran his hand over his fair forelock and enquired of the steward: "Have you any grapefruit?"

"What do you mean, sir?" The steward was all attention at once.

"It's a sort of large lemon, young man, American manufacture—it's eaten with or without sugar. Some people are mad about it."

"Never heard of it, sir," said the steward.

"No grapefruit to be had," translated Otto.

Mr. Hunter was indignant, but he did not find it unpleasant to be able to remain indignant. Yesterday there had been no ice for his soda-water—the kitchen could not spare the ice, he had been told. And that with the dearest tickets on the dearest express in Europe. A Pullman they called the thing. Yes, unhygienic, finger-marked brass handles, dusty upholstery, not even a radio: a fine Pullman. No! Bad organization! Europe!

"Here's Mr. Haymaker," said Otto, and pushed aside his newspapers.

"Good morning, young men," was tall Haymaker's greeting. He had a much more refined air than his friend. But then he also had a pair of genial dark eyes inherited from his Irish ancestry. "Hunter, you haven't slept. You're looking yellow. Come along and have breakfast."

"No, no breakfast for me," grumbled Hunter. "You go and take your rolls with coffee. I've had enough, with my constipation yesterday. Grapefruit isn't to be had."

"When we're in Vienna you can eat as much grapefruit as you like," said Haymaker consolingly. "Can't he, Wernizek?"

"Probably not. We're more expert at *mehlspeisen*; but the big hotels provide everything foreigners want."

"Nonsense," said Mr. Hunter irritably. "I'm not here to be looked after and exploited, and then be laughed at when my back's turned. In Vienna I want to do as the Viennese do, even if I have to suffer hunger for a week."

"It isn't even a week now," said Otto grimly. "You stayed in Paris two days too long. The Rotarians have been busy at their congress long since."

"Yes, old boy," grinned Haymaker. "In Paris you wanted to do as the Parisians do—of course that takes time. . . ."

This gibe, which he had heard several times before,

Mr. Hunter allowed to pass without protest. He himself knew how much truth there was in it. Paris, the Paris for which the hotel porter had given him the whispered instructions, was not so very interesting after all. New York could teach Paris a thing or two. Mr. Hunter had only moderately enjoyed his expeditions of discovery into the Paris demi-monde. Actually they had been no more to him than a pretext enabling him to remain in the neighborhood of Haymaker and his secretary until they had got in their pockets the contract with their French guest conductor and were prepared to travel on with him to Vienna.

For it must be confessed Mr. Hunter did not like the idea of traveling further entirely alone. From however great a height he might look down upon this feckless Europe, he felt very uncertain of his ground. In the first place, he spoke only American, and even that with difficulty. Actually he was well acquainted only with his own technical language, the language of his cable factory; and what use was that to him in Belgium, France, Germany, Austria, if he really wanted to see something of the life in those countries, as he had after all been instructed to do by the Rotary Club of Midland? Of course, he was greatly helped by his first-class film camera: for an amateur, he really did use it very cleverly. But a film was, after all, only a dumb, speechless recorder. More than that, he had begun to observe that in Europe the importance of things was not to be measured by their audibility or visibility, and that therefore one had to understand the more: but to understand was impossible to him unless there was someone present to explain.

When Haymaker had ceased to snigger, Hunter said in self-defense: "However that may be, I've learnt something in Paris by my system."

Mr. Haymaker sniggered afresh, and louder; but Mr. Hunter turned to Otto. "Can't you give me a few hints about Vienna, Wernizek?"

Otto von Wernizek sat up straight. "Oh, yes. But to begin with there are several things you must bear in mind. Vienna is an imperial city without an emperor. In fact, it is nothing more than a pleasant memory. Something like an empty oyster shell. Of course one may regard a shell as a pretty object; but I prefer a good, fresh, just-opened Huitre de Zélande. You've just been supping in Paris: so I'm afraid our empty oyster shell will leave you pretty indifferent."

Mr. Haymaker slapped his knee. "You're a fine chap, Wernizek. As soon as we're in Amsterdam I'll treat you to two dozen Dutch oysters. And you're quite right too—but not only about Vienna. The whole of Europe, man, is an emptied oyster shell. I'm here for the seventh time. The first time I was over was in 1898. I saw the oyster when it was still fresh, but it did not last very long. And now the supper is quite definitely over."

38

Haymaker would have liked to revel a little longer in his vision of the European oyster, but Otto interrupted him. Otto von Wernizek had heard himself holding forth once more, and was delighted. Three years of curt, succinct Americanism had dropped from him as he approached Passau. He smiled, and went on: "That doesn't alter the fact that you'll be able to take some very pretty photos in Vienna. The Spanish Riding School, for instance—it's being kept up by some old comrades of mine. It actually brings in more to the treasury than the Opera. Then there are the young girls along the Ring, and the Corpus Christi procession, although of course that's no longer what it was, either. The Rotarians will show you the museums and so forth, but you're not allowed to use your camera there. For the rest, there's not much that'll interest you."

"Nonsense," said Mr. Haymaker, laughing. "If there was no more to your beloved Vienna than that, you'd not be on such tenterhooks to get home."

"I was merely giving Mr. Hunter a few hints as to what we can offer an American in the way of things to be seen. If I could show him round the city myself, I should probably be able to weave a beautiful legend round every building that we met, including our unhappy Ministry of Finance—oh, yes, the pretty palace of Prince Eugene, divine baroque—but all that means nothing. I'm a Wernizek-Bolnanyi and I love the city.

It's far better that he should go out alone with his camera. Then he'll get a detached impression."

"Couldn't you spare me a day?" asked Mr. Hunter. He himself noticed that there was a deferential sound about this, and was surprised to hear himself addressing Mr. Haymaker's secretary in that tone. But even Haymaker appeared to treat his secretary differently on this journey—he had actually once gone so far as to say "Mr. von Wernizek."

"I've received six days' leave from the boss," said Otto, smiling, "and I've made up my mind to plunge right under. I shall get you and Mr. Haymaker into a good hotel. The rest the Rotarians must do."

"Oho," Haymaker broke in. "We can't have that, young man. You've six days' leave of the eight. That leaves two over for me. I must have your address, for when I want you I want to be able to ring you up."

"Can't be done," said Otto. "I'm staying with an aunt in the depths of a remote quarter. No telephone in the whole house. If you want me, you'll have to fetch me yourself, or send a taxi."

"But why won't you have a decent room in my hotel?" asked Haymaker in astonishment. He was not really a bad boss and would not be likely to give needless trouble to a man on his holiday. Wernizek knew that too. How could the fellow prefer a back street to a room in a hotel with bathroom attached? Generally Haymaker understood Europeans very well, but this was abnormal.

40

The train was gradually slowing down. The door of the compartment was jerked open. A passport official stuck his hand inside, hastily examined the American passports. Then he inspected the Austrian one: Von Wernizek-Bolnanyi, Otto—eyes: gray—hair: light brown—nose: straight—height: 5′ 5″—birthmark under left ear—born October 1, 1898. He made a deep bow in Otto's direction, and passed on.

"I prefer not to live in an hotel in my own city," said Otto quietly. The train stopped: Passau.

Mr. Haymaker and his friend strolled through the train. Mr. Hunter was bent upon adding to his pictures one of the Austrian engine that had just been hitched on. He felt himself grow as he thought of the impression these incapable plaything machines of diverse nationality would make by contrast with his photographs of the powerful American giants that maintained connection between two oceans. He took a picture of the puffing engine while a train-cleaner watched him with friendly interest. Then a close-up of a patch of rust on the connecting-rod, and then a second close-up of the thin, graying driver who was filling his pipe with an air of satisfaction as he leaned over the iron railing. But as he did so, his smile became so humiliatingly superior to his surroundings that the train-cleaner turned away and resumed his work.

"You were right a moment ago," said Mr. Hunter.

41

"It's all over here. What businesslike manager would keep such old people in his service?"

"Presumably a management that's set against too high pension costs," suggested Haymaker. "Yes, old man, I too think it's all over here. I didn't want to affront Wernizek a moment ago—such people are always more easily hurt than you imagine. But I don't mind telling you. Do you know what his Europe is, Hunter? The whole of this Europe, with all its important buildings and people and ideas and institutions? A museum, Hunter. A great historical museum. And badly organized at that. They haven't even labeled the exhibits. Each person can think what he likes of them."

DANIEL JONATHAN watched his grandfather enter the secretariat. For quite half a minute he continued to look at the closed doors. Then he stepped into the shabby hired Mercedes and went to fetch Peter Ladislaus, as he had been instructed. But first he had some errands to do. Bread, wine, ether, Julius's instrument case. Two revolvers, cartridges.

Yes, revolvers. It was a difficult commission on this particular day, when all the papers were writing about the shindies, to buy revolvers unobtrusively. But it had to be done.

At half-past eight he was standing in Julius's room —Julius had given him the key. He found his instrument case under the divan. Bread, wine, and ether he had obtained. Then he bought a small French revolver in the dignified gun shop in the Kohlmarkt. Of course he had slipped his student's badge behind the lapel of his coat. At ten to nine he bought a second revolver from Süssholz in the Griechenstrasse. He had never been in the shop before, although he had often heard of it. Süssholz sold a great deal to students. He had boxing gloves, fencing foils, underwear, canoes—and what not. And everything by installments. Süssholz saw that this young man was not accustomed to handling revolvers. Further, he wanted to pay cash. Süssholz felt vague scruples. He was himself a Jew. But then a shopkeeper keeps a shop in order to sell.

As he wrapped the packet of cartridges neatly in soft paper and, putting the revolver with it, passed an elastic band round the two, Süssholz remarked: "I should leave the revolver at home for the time being. These are no times for going to college with a revolver in one's pocket."

Daniel shrugged his shoulders. "I don't go to college. I'm a journalist."

Süssholz looked at him with polite incredulity, and then rolled the double packet in a pink paper covering. The addition of a narrow black-and-white tape to secure it gave it a completely innocuous appearance. Daniel paid. He had had no idea that revolvers cost so much. But little Weissenstein had provided the money.

At five to nine, he passed the Tower of St. Stephen's without glancing at it. At five past he was in sight of the Matteottihof. If only Ladislaus were at home.

He raced across the little square. A small band of unemployed were lounging listlessly round the pool with the sculptured group of good-natured bears.

"Is Ladislaus at home?" he enquired of a man whose face he knew from Communist meetings.

"I'll go and have a look," said somebody, and

44

slouched up the concrete staircase. Then a hand beckoned from a window above, and a voice called: "At home."

"Can he come with me at once?" asked Daniel. There was no answer. Everything was all right then; Ladislaus would come.

Two minutes later, Peter Ladislaus was standing on the steps. He had put on a woolen scarf, which filled Daniel with astonishment, for the broiling June sun was pouring down over the houses, even though it was only nine o'clock, and the air already smelt close. But Ladislaus seemed to be wedded to this scarf—he always wore it at meetings: he was tubercular and chilly.

"What's up?" he asked. He was not sure of Daniel's name—he met so many young people of that sort. He was one of the few Communists at the university and held, nevertheless, the position of an undisputed leader. He was nearly thirty, and still made no effort to take his degree. He had worked in Moscow in various offices for several periods. He had a tawny yellow face and lanky black hair—due, no doubt, to his Mongolian descent. He was ready for everything and everyone, and when it was a question of furthering the Communist cause, he did not spare his person. Daniel had a great deal of respect for Ladislaus, although he did not always agree with what he heard him say at meetings. Daniel was still not a

45

regular member of the Communist party, and deep in his heart he felt a vague aversion to Ladislaus.

"The car's over there. I'll tell you as we drive along." Daniel pushed Ladislaus forward: he had to be back with the others in Laxenburg by ten o'clock. Those were his instructions.

Meanwhile the first touring car had deposited its load of sightseers on the little square. For foreigners, these days, were taking an interest in the new architecture of the municipality of Vienna, just as they used to be interested in the Wurstel-Prater and the Prince Eugene Monument. On the whole, the new architecture did not please them. They had aesthetic objections, and were not sufficiently receptive to the social enthusiasm that had built these stately barracks. They stood in the little square looking up with some perplexity at the buildings piled up round them.

"This is the Matteottihof," began the guide, "built in 1926-7, designed by the building department of the Vienna municipality. The costs were met by the building fund . . ."

"Stop!" cried a fat Bavarian. "Who is Matteotti?"

The leader of the touring party, a right-minded, sturdily built Social Democrat, stood amazed at this lack of knowledge. He was about to explain, searching his mind for the necessary data. Matteotti was murdered in . . . God—when was it? Then he thought of a way out. "Matteotti was a martyr for socialism," he declared, and stood listening dubiously

46

to the pathetic reverberation of his words that remained hanging above his indifferent public.

At that moment, Ladislaus passed the group. "Matteotti was an Italian Social Democrat who was murdered by the Fascists in 1924. Hundreds of Socialists and Communists were murdered at that time," he said stiffly. He had a scientific aversion to romanticism and phrases. The fat Bavarian looked up and about him. Ladislaus's yellow face did not particularly meet with his approval.

The unemployed were hanging about the pool, watching the show. One of them spat from two yards away into the water. An English girl shrank back, then laughed pleasantly in the direction of her guide, and said: "Look at the small bear! Isn't it delicious?"

"Beautiful animal sculpture by Hanna Gärdtner: she-bear with young," explained the guide, and avoided the glances of the unemployed, who stood there visibly despising him.

"Can you eat that?" asked one. Ladislaus's eyes lit up with a burning glow. He stood still.

"Let's get on, please," urged Daniel. "I'm in a hurry."

And so the over-driven but willing Mercedes set off in haste for Laxenburg at a quarter past nine, spitting blue fumes for the best part of a mile.

"Well?" asked Ladislaus.

Daniel drew himself up behind the steering-wheel.

47

He had a detailed report to give. "Fritz Weissenstein has been found," he said.

"Oh, yes." The report left Ladislaus indifferent. "That was in the paper last night. Mutilated, hey? But he'll recover from that all right."

Daniel swerved to avoid a lorry. "Mutilated? Yes, I suppose you could call it that—they've castrated him." He clenched his teeth. The car rushed down an incline, hooting.

Ladislaus whistled softly. "I've expected something of the kind for a long time," he said.

"Expected?"

"Yes. That was always done in Russia in the old days when a Jew carried on with a Christian girl. Only they went about it in a less civilized way—at least, I read in the paper something to the effect that the wound had been expertly bandaged."

Daniel suddenly felt his unreasoning aversion to Ladislaus welling up from unsuspected depths into his throat. But what could it be?

"But now just tell me plainly what I've got to do with all this." He was only moderately well disposed towards the Austrians. They were a romantic people who knew nothing of organization. Much too emotional.

Daniel was now sitting quietly behind the steering-wheel again—but he had moved a little to one side: Ladislaus's hand had been resting against his coat.

"Fritz Weissenstein is lying in the Rothschild Hospital. We know what happened from the assistant. That doesn't get into the papers, of course. He seems to have been dealt with under a narcotic. No one knows by whom or where. He himself refuses to say anything."

"Of course," said Ladislaus, nodding. "What have the police to do with that? They only get busy over such things when they want to find out something about you. Otherwise they leave you lying quietly in the mire."

"Yesterday morning they found Fritz in his own car outside his girl's house. . . ."

"Yes, yes. That was in Döbling, Hartackerstrasse. What was in the paper I know already."

Daniel puckered his eyebrows. His eyes looked ahead down the long straight road, through the flat green country. The trees swayed past them. He could be in Laxenburg in a quarter of an hour, in plenty of time. Strange that there should be people like this Peter Ladislaus with brains that worked automatically, even when such appalling things happened as had now occurred to Fritz. But Ladislaus knew Fritz. Why was he not appalled by this news, like any other ordinary person? Why did he sit there now like a general cross-examining an adjutant? Yes, what had Ladislaus to do with all this?

But then Daniel remembered that for the last two days he had been under orders from Hermann Julius, who had had Ladislaus summoned—he himself therefore had neither to think nor question any more. He added: "Fritz Weissenstein's brother came to us yesterday morning . . ."

"Who is us?" queried Ladislaus.

"The circle. We call it the circle. That sounds ethical. It's better to choose a name that doesn't attract attention in case one forgets oneself on occasion when others are present. We've met for a long time now, just to jaw about a thousand and one things—but since Monday when they threw Walter out of the window of the Aula—"

"I know, I know," said Ladislaus.

"We've constituted ourselves into a defense group organized in a really practical manner."

"Won't you mention a few names?" enquired Ladislaus.

Julius is the leader. You will see him in a moment. Weissenstein's youngest brother is there also. And I of course. For other names you can ask Julius. I mustn't mention them of course, not even to you."

"Very well," said Ladislaus.

"Little Weissenstein, Fritz's youngest brother, came yesterday morning to Julius to say that Fritz had been found, and how." Daniel swallowed. Beneath his stiff bearing he was a shivering lump of horror and despair. But he was under discipline; he had taken his oath with the others; he was reporting a case. "Julius immediately sent to enquire of the doctors who was to be suspected. Yesterday afternoon, Rolff—"

"The Sozi?" asked Ladislaus.

"Yes, and a decent fellow." Daniel himself felt how stiffly his hand clutched the steering-wheel.

"Certainly," said Ladislaus with a smile. "A decent fellow."

"Yesterday afternoon Rolff sent word that Rasser and Derresch . . ."

"The brother of Olga Derresch, the girl outside whose house Fritz was found in his car."

"You know everything," said Daniel, and felt small.

"Go on with your story," said Ladislaus.

"Rolff sent word that Rasser and Derresch, who live together, hadn't been back to their room for several days, nor had they been seen at the demonstrations in the street; and that last year Rasser had had an affair with Olga. Furthermore, both of them are almost ready for their surgical."

"There's something in that," said Ladislaus, "but now I should really like to know what I've got to do with this childish business."

Daniel could have groaned, but of course he did not. "Julius only told me to tell you these facts before we reached Laxenburg. Last night we kidnaped Rasser and Derresch. Nothing could have been easier. They'd rented a week-end hut somewhere in Klosterneuburg on the Danube. Yesterday afternoon we discovered them as they were lying sunning themselves, but we preferred to wait till night-time. Of course they've a superb alibi: all the sunbathers can see you during the day as you lie there or swim, and nobody bothers about what anybody else does at night. They could have murdered Fritz Weissenstein while their neighbors thought they were having fun with some girl or other. But last night we got hold of them and brought them to Laxenburg."

"Splendid, splendid!" said Ladislaus. "Which hotel did you choose?"

Daniel sat bolt upright. "Excuse me, we're not children. They're in a summer-house in the Schloss Laxenburg park where not a soul goes nowadays. Julius knew the place. He camped in the neighborhood last summer, and never saw a soul. It's a little empty pavilion, and lies more than two miles behind the main building."

"I see," said Ladislaus. "This is how things stand then: you've got in Schloss Laxenburg, where, by the way, a proper watch is kept, a couple of Nazi students of good family for whom the whole of Vienna will be looking within twenty-four hours. Added to which, you simply don't know yet whether they had anything to do with the Weissenstein case. Congratulations!"

"Pardon me." Daniel began to feel unwell. "We know Fritz was found outside Olga Derresch's door and that she had sent Rasser packing and spent the Easter holiday in Munich with Fritz Weissenstein. We know further that Derresch is the greatest Jew hater at the Academy. Do you think he'd have deprived himself of the pleasure of beating up the Jewish students if he hadn't had something else to do?"

"Yes, my dear friend. That's all very well. And yet, believe me, the sooner you get rid of those boys the better. Do they know who you are?"

"Of course not. They're still packed up just as we took them away last night, neatly rolled in their blankets, with a tent canvas round them."

"Ah, well, we shall see," said Ladislaus. "I'm still not clear as to what I've got to do with all this. Fritz isn't a member of the Communist party, and you didn't seek my advice when you founded your circle. Only Julius is one of us so far as I know."

Daniel had changed into second gear. The car shivered and ascended an incline. He could not understand either why Julius had wanted to summon Ladislaus. But he had his orders. Julius was the leader.

"I've no time for students' private quarrels," continued Ladislaus, "and if you really want to constitute a defense group, you must be able to act independently in individual cases; and, if I see clearly, your aspirations don't go further than the individual case."

But yes, whatever he said Daniel's aspirations did go further, much further. He longed for a world in which men would behave as brothers, in which the sorrow of one man would be the sorrow of another, and all would be bound together by a great joy in the beauty of life. He longed for sun, for beauty, for love—above all, he longed passionately, and did not know that he longed with the inevitable longing of his own twenty-year-old heart.

He would have liked to justify himself to Ladislaus. He could not endure contempt when he felt this fiery longing streaming through him; and at the same time he concealed his longing, though with difficulty, under the matter-of-fact air he wore like a mask over an agitated soul ready for any sacrifice. As he sought for words that would sum up all this for Ladislaus, Ladislaus asked: "How far are we still from Laxenburg?"

"About ten minutes."

"Then shut up. I've something here I must read."

Daniel clenched his jaws together: he had suddenly realized that his teeth would chatter if he were not careful. It was a strange sensation. He had never experienced anything like it before, and suddenly it was clear to him that he was afraid. 'Am I really afraid?' he thought, and probed into himself. He knew he was afraid, but could not feel where the fear lay. Ladislaus was sitting quietly beside him engrossed in a bundle of stenciled sheets—statistics, Daniel could see. The car whirred without any untoward noises; the road was straight and empty. Yonder in Laxenburg Julius was waiting and would decide with Ladislaus what was to happen next. He himself had no decisions to make. There was really no reason why, just at that moment, he should be afraid. How came it, then, that suddenly he felt so inexpressibly heavy and at the same time conscious of a quivering though painless cramp in all his muscles, an impotent trembling of his arms and legs? 'Nerves?' he thought. 'Gott im Himmel, I'm not an old maid,' and was annoyed beyond measure. Besides, it was as clear to him as it had been yesterday and the day before that he belonged to a defense group and was under military discipline. He knew Fritz Weissenstein had been treacherously maimed for life, and that the circle must avenge him. He knew he had declared in his oath that he would assume all responsibility for each collective act of the circle until Hermann Julius disbanded it. He knew perfectly well that he had taken the oath with all its implications and had intended to take it in bitter earnest—and yet his fainthearted body was now leaving him in the lurch: it was shivering and trembling, and if he were not careful his teeth would chatter audibly. 'Himmel! What a booby I am,' thought Daniel, and tried to dig his heels into the mat under his feet.

"Here we are," said Ladislaus. In spite of his interest in statistics, he had observed sooner than Daniel that they had reached Laxenburg. 'Remarkable,' thought Daniel, and felt himself doubly unhappy in his manifest inadequacy. But they were already in the by-way. Daniel swerved round a group of trees, and brought the car onto the sandpath. The soft road was full of ruts and holes. He needed all his attention for the car. His natural gift for driving, however, helped him safely over the difficulties—it really was a gift. Fritz Weissenstein, who had taught him to drive, called it a miracle. He smiled as he dodged or overcame hole after hole. The old Mercedes groaned, but did submissively what was expected of her. And when Daniel stopped in front of the summer-house he observed that he had ceased to tremble.

Hermann Julius came running up. He was a heavy, ash-blond North German. His small gray eyes lay deep in their sockets. He had a flat square back to his head, and over his broad lips there played a persistent laugh that was not merry. "Hand over your bread! We're fainting with hunger," he ordered Daniel, who gave him the bag of rolls and the bottle of white wine. Ladislaus stepped out, and looked round him, then sought shelter behind a group of fir-trees and beckoned to Julius.

"Go right in," the latter ordered Daniel, as he followed Ladislaus. The bread and the bottle he kept. He chewed and swallowed and chewed with the natural satisfaction of a ruminant. Ladislaus heard, and smiled ironically. He did not know what appetite was: that was owing to t.b.

Behind the small fir-trees, they squatted down together on a couple of oak trunks. Julius felt in the bag for a fourth caraway-seed roll, but having apparently finished them, he started on the sweet rolls. Ladislaus could not bear to watch him any longer. He stared up at the oak leaves.

"What was your plan?" he asked at last.

"I want to give Rasser and Derresch a little warning. For the other gentry too," said Julius. "I've had my instrument case fetched and some ether."

Ladislaus sniffed audibly. "You're nothing more than a common-or-garden little sadist, Julius. God Almighty—what am I doing here with you lot? The whole university is a children's nursery gone mad, and here I'm sitting among you as confidential adviser. You're a Communist, by God, and you don't know any better than to busy yourself with a students' shindy over a rich Jew boy, and you've fetched me for that. But couldn't you have left me out of it, you big fool?"

"Oh, no," said Julius, "not at all. I'm not even the very smallest little fool. Of course I have my own private account to settle with Rasser, but it isn't for that that I need you. I only wanted to bring you into touch with this group. It was a good opportunity to put them in the position to compromise themselves in your presence. There really are one or two useful elements among them."

"It's not worth while," said Ladislaus decisively. "What do I want with a handful of whipper-snappers whom I can only use when it's a case of beating up somebody or other? If you could bring me a gang of railway workers or some non-commissioned officers, or even a printer from the *Arbeiter Zeitung*. They're all people I could recommend for a tough job of work. But what am I to do with a son of Weissenstein the banker?"

"The compromised son of an influential father is a precious possession," said Julius in a lecturing tone. "But it's just as you like. In any case, they're already sufficiently compromised for my special purpose."

Ladislaus's broad nostrils had turned sallow. "Stop!" said he. "You've had me summoned. I've therefore something to say. For the time being, you're not going to carry out your special purpose. There's to be no settling of private accounts that can be put to the charge of the Communists later on. Now I'm here, I'm in charge. Tell those boys to come here. Who was the colt that drove me?"

"Daniel Jonathan, a third-year law student, with a noble disposition. A budding martyr. Really, Ladislaus, you're an ungrateful dog. I only sent that boy to you because I wanted to please you. He's one of your sort—an idealist who's got something in him. If you were to lift your little finger you'd have him body and soul."

"I should like to know why you became a Communist," said Ladislaus.

"I've explained that to you before, but you don't seem able to believe me: because my father lost his

58

job in Hanover through those Nazi gentry. And I've
got to try and finish my studies here in Vienna as
cheaply as I can. I'm not imagining a kind of film-
land city of the future, Ladislaus. I only know that I
intend to get this accursed world under my feet."
Julius's eternal laugh now lay, disquietingly lacking
in gaiety, about his lips. With a sharp tap he knocked
off the neck of his bottle of white wine against a tree
trunk.

"That's probably only a different conception of tac-
tics, for the time being at any rate," said Ladislaus,
as he coughed violently into his handkerchief. Julius
ate his sixth roll, waiting for Ladislaus to recover,
and when he saw that Ladislaus was sitting up straight
again, he went to fetch Daniel and little Weissenstein.

Poor Weissenstein was as white as a sheet; but
then he had had to help look for his brother for two
days, and had not eaten anything since the night before. Even Julius noticed it, and gave him the last
two rolls.

"You've still got your prisoners all right?" enquired Ladislaus.

"No getting away," Julius declared. "Rolled up in
their blankets and tightly roped."

"Ah, well, come and sit down," said Ladislaus.

Daniel felt in his pocket. He still had to deliver the
revolvers. He produced the trim little parcels, laid
them down on a heap of moss, and untied the papers,
which the watchful Ladislaus systematically stuck

59

into his pocket. When, however, the gleaming little revolvers appeared Ladislaus jumped up swearing, his thin body trembling under the explosion.

"This is the limit, you stupid beasts! Must you people in Vienna be theatrical in everything? Conspiracy under the oaks! Oath upon weapons! It's enough to make one weep. Newly bought—this morning, I suppose, eh?"

Julius looked on with a sly little laugh. "Daniel bought them. He's sure to have been careful. Weren't you?"

"I don't think Süssholz knows me," said Daniel sullenly.

"You mustn't think: you must know," roared Ladislaus. "But who are these revolvers for, Julius? You have yours, haven't you?"

"For these two good boys who must have something in hand in case of need. When we begin to cross-examine Rasser and Derresch, we shall have to unfasten them a bit first. We've pulled the blankets over their heads. They can't speak like that."

"Right. Now I know enough," said Ladislaus. "Will you people kindly listen a moment? There's nothing to cross-examine about. It's clear enough that these two idiots played this hooligan's trick on Fritz Weissenstein. . . ." Young Weissenstein, outraged, raised a hand, but Ladislaus proceeded calmly. "They deserve something—and if they don't get it this time, they will some other. But it's absolutely unnecessary

60

you should all go to jail for it, and it's as plain as a pikestaff that you will if you go on muddling through in the amusing and romantic way you've behaved so far. Rolff knows about it, and he's a decent Social Democrat. You may therefore get into trouble in that direction."

Daniel and young Weissenstein were standing a little dumbfounded, like recruits before a sergeant. They waited, however, confident that Julius would give a decisive answer. Julius was the leader. In his hands they had laid their oath. But Julius sat on his tree trunk gulping down the last drop of wine from the bottle, very carefully so as not to cut himself on the broken neck.

"Well, now," proceeded Ladislaus, "all those two inside know is that they've been kidnaped by someone unknown. I hope you haven't let them hear your voices."

"Of course not," said young Weissenstein. "Julius forbade us to."

Ladislaus nodded approval. "Then that's all right. Now we must just look in to see if there's anything lying about—give me that bag, Weissenstein, and you keep hold of this bottle. Don't forget the neck, Julius —and then we'll drive like hell through Mödling towards Vienna, this time avoiding the Laxenburger Allee at all costs. . . ."

"And we just leave them lying here?" asked young Weissenstein.

"And we just leave them lying here," confirmed Ladislaus. "It's the only thing we can do. If what Julius says is true, and nobody ever comes here, then they're in for it; but that's their risk. If on the other hand they're properly searched for—and I assure you that Councilor Rasser will have his son searched for —then they'll get off with a fright. Now then—forward march."

Julius took the wheel. Daniel sat next to Ladislaus on the back seat. He was for the moment completely empty of all thought. He was only aware with astonishment that he was on the way back to Vienna. Soon he would be back in the Luftbadgasse and would be able to go to bed, to sleep. It was a wonderfully simple ending to the adventure of these last days— but was it really an end? Daniel noted that he did not really believe it to be an end. He did not quite know why. He could at this moment in his consciousness turn nothing into thoughts or words, and now there was this difficulty again of getting his teeth to rest quietly upon each other. That required a good deal of concentration.

From time to time, however, a few disconnected words pressed themselves upon his attention. He chased them away, and there they were again, plain ordinary words: 'What are you to do now? What are you to do now?' It was very tiring for him to be on his guard so that no one should see the trembling of his cheeks, and at the same time to shake off these words. But then Daniel was very weary. He lay against the upholstered cushions, lurching sideways with every swerve of the car. But he was careful not to touch Ladislaus. Ladislaus, who was again engrossed in his stenciled statistics.

An hour later, the Mercedes was standing once more in the hired garage where it belonged.

"Had some fun?" asked the garage man.

"Oh, fun enough," muttered Julius, "but those accursed girls do cost a lot."

"They're worth it, sir," said the man, laughing as he thumped the departing Julius in the back.

Ladislaus was already standing on the pavement. He had slipped his papers in his pocket, and was winding his scarf about his neck. "Just drop in this afternoon at about four," he said to Daniel. "I've one or two books on Soviet law that a jurist ought to read." He put out his hand to Daniel. Curiously enough, it was still as damp and chilly as it had been a couple of hours ago; but now to Daniel's confusion it left behind it an unexpectedly pleasant impression.

LUFTBADGASSE No. 12 was now in bustling morning trim. At Hodl's of course there was already a busy coming and going, but the other flats were also in the thick of the day that had long since started. On the first floor the poodle, acting upon Herr Friedemann's instructions, was yapping a peddler from the door, while ex-Counselor of Justice Kerner was dragging himself up the stairs carrying an old carpet he had been beating as free as possible of dust in the courtyard. Herr Friedemann hastily shut the front door—it is better not to look at a man who has sunk so low as Herr Kerner. To do so might involve one in difficulties with him.

On the second-floor landing, right opposite Maria Ritter's front door, three of the Bergmann children, all starched and white, were playing busily. Later on, at their grandparents' festival, they were to act as flower-strewers. The front door was their "stand." They were enjoying their free morning to the full. Their delight reverberated uninterruptedly up and down the whole staircase. Maria Ritter's housekeeper, the diligent Josephine, who was already mixing in the kitchen the paste for one of her famous *Kirschenstrudels*, heard the noise well enough, but contrary to her custom did not rush out to give the neighbor's children the reprimand they deserved. She had a secret hope that Maria might be awakened somewhat earlier than usual by the hubbub, and this, for many reasons, would not have displeased her today; but in the inner room where Maria lay everything remained quiet. There the day had not begun yet.

And so at ten o'clock Josephine drew back the curtains in Maria Ritter's bedroom, and pulled up the Venetian blinds between the double windows. That was her regular habit at this time, for if she did not do it Maria would certainly sleep on till twelve o'clock, and how could Josephine help Maria at her toilet while the mid-day meal was cooking?

Maria gave a last smothered snore. Then she put her hands over her eyes and crept further under the blankets; but she snored no more.

"Gnädige Frau," said Josephine, and threw back the bedclothes. "Gnädige Frau, it's past ten," and true enough the white daylight was now shining into the room, and Josephine, who had been up since six o'clock, had reason to be displeased with Maria, who could not wake even at ten. Still, she exercised patience and ceased her endeavors to summon Maria back to the workaday world. Maria slept with such complete abandon, her old face lay so completely relaxed in dreams, that Josephine stopped there watching her, hesitant as one is reluctant to lift an infant from a warm cradle.

Josephine knew Maria's face under many aspects. She had seen it for the first time forty years ago under the little rococo cap of "Rosine," and from the very first moment she had loved it with a warm fondness. It was so utterly different from her own narrow, bony, South German type. From the gallery where she was enjoying "The Barber" on one of her free evenings, she had admired the round, agreeable but never frivolous countenance of the greatest coloratura singer of the century, had surrendered to the jubilant warbling voice, had found release and gone home happy. Next day she had spontaneously offered her services to that large, foolish child, Maria Ritter, who, according to what she heard later from her colleagues of the dressing-room, was robbed and defrauded by her servants on all sides. Since that time, she had looked after and spoilt Maria, despite the fact that she was fifteen years younger than her mistress, reprimanded her and brought her up, waved and cut her reddish-blonde hair according to the requirements of changing fashion, massaged her ample, comely body and generally taken delight in her presence. She had been entirely happy with and satisfied by Maria, and she was so still: only she never cared to admit it.

Now that Maria was seventy-four, and her body had fallen into decline, now that she had, moreover, although pensioned, to live frugally, according to her standards, Josephine had found in Maria her most genuine reasons for existing. Suppose Josephine were not there: life would be unthinkable for Maria, would it not?

And so Josephine stood by Maria's bedstead and looked down on the lusterless reddish hair that Maria would not yet allow to grow gray, on the swollen, blue-veined nose, on the sunken yellow-red cheeks; and she loved Maria just as she was, with an almost painful devotion. But that she would never admit even to herself.

"Gnädige Frau," said Josephine, "you really must get up. There are letters too."

That was the magic word that brought Maria back to daily reality. It worked as infallibly as the cold sponge that Maria's mother had been in the habit of calling to her aid many years ago when Maria had slept past the opening hour of the Conservatoire. Maria Ritter came to life again when she saw the post, and truth to tell it was often a very pleasant little packet of letters that the postman had to deliver. Maria possessed old and faithful correspondents all over the globe. In every part of the world lived people who had admired her and loved her, and who from gratitude for a beautiful fairy-tale evening had laid at her feet their full, entranced hearts. Old ladies and gentlemen they were now, but in their time the enthusiastic culture-bearers of the pre-war world.

Maria Ritter belonged to a time when a great singer did not require a publicity manager, nor a secretary. She had faithfully answered all her letters—or left them unanswered. She had chosen her friends herself and had tolerated no other counselor in her love affairs than the longing of her warm body and her joyous heart. Many an aged English gentleman, many a white-haired Parisian aristocrat, many a forgotten conductor or composer, smiled blissfully as they filled the sheets with the decorative, neat flourishes of an antiquated calligraphy and addressed them to Luftbadgasse No. 12, Vienna. Many others too, from a warm, romantic gratitude, continued to link their insignificant private lives with hers. These epistles, now, alas, diminishing in number, from her former admirers of both sexes were the last reward of Maria Ritter's beautiful life as a faithful artist. They came from all the capitals of the civilized world, and brought her the indestructible devotion and gratitude of a generation that had known how to enjoy a beautiful fiction.

Maria Ritter had become a legend while she was still on earth. When she reached her seventieth birthday, newspaper readers said: "Oh, is she still alive?" She had already joined the band of Paganini and Taglione, of Eleonora Duse and Jenny Lind. But that of course applied only to newspaper readers. She herself felt that she was still very much alive and not more than fifty or so. That is to say, as the world imagines a woman of fifty who has the summer of her life behind her must feel. For when Maria Ritter actually celebrated her fiftieth birthday (without publicity) she was a most beautiful, opulent, full-blown rose, and felt five-and-thirty.

Now, truth to tell, she was a shade too heavy, and the voice—yes—she had been unable to keep that. When in 1916 the management of the Opera offered her a pension as delicately as possible, she could not work up in her honest heart the necessary agitation to unleash a theatrical scandal. Fifty-eight, after all, was more than the limit for a coloratura singer at the Vienna Opera House. But an increase in her pension she did in the end obtain, through the interposition of the Archduke Karl, who gave it as his opinion that it would be a national scandal if Maria Ritter had to advertise as a teacher of singing. Besides, she would have been a complete failure. Maria Ritter's voice was unique, but her theoretical knowledge was nil. She had remained all her life the airy, irresponsible singing bird that Direktor Ker had discovered at Father Ritter's sausage shop.

Yes, and it was not to be gainsaid that now the bird was rather stiff and stout. In the mornings Josephine had to slip Maria's slippers on her feet before she allowed herself to slide out of bed. Josephine also had to help her in the kitchen where hung the hot-water shower, and where every morning for a full hour Maria washed and tended her body, formerly so precious and now the source of so much heartache to her.

For Josephine, Maria's body had no mysteries—

indeed, she was as familiar with all Maria's concerns as was her mistress. Josephine had read through all the letters long before Maria was awake.

"It's a good post today," she said, and handed Maria the tray with her coffee and rolls. The letters she laid upon the table as a bait for Maria, who liked very much to lie down again after her breakfast.

"From whom?" asked Maria.

"Mr. Lytton of Chicago. Baroness Märzenburg, with a very nice snapshot of her pushing her grandson in his pram. Carlo Perrucci sends an account of a performance at the Scala where a new-comer's 'Angelina' is compared with yours twenty years ago."

"Yes, Rossini always was my forte," said Maria, "but those disgusting newspaper villains ought not always to slaughter young people with our old reputations. I was young myself once. I know what it is, and don't you believe they can really hear whether there's anything in a child like that or not—they only want to show that years ago they saw Maria Ritter." Maria had a great deal of professional loyalty, always had had. She was a good comrade, even to the chorus-girls.

"Still," she said, "something occurs to me. Talking of young people. A little later you must go to that boy at the back. I've a seat for Thibaud this evening. He can have it. I've promised the Hodls to go to their celebration, and you don't care for concerts."

"I'm going to the golden wedding too, of course,"

said Josephine, offended. She was still not cured of her servant's pride, and did not like to be left at home if it was possible to appear anywhere in Maria's company.

"Of course you're coming too," said Maria soothingly. "Perhaps I'll sing a bit there. Hodl asked me so pressingly." Poor Maria! She was really rather flattered by the request, even though she did also smile within herself in self-mockery. She was grateful to be allowed to sing once more before an audience.

"Now give me the letters," said Maria.

"Hadn't you better get up?" insisted Josephine. "I must go to the Naschmarkt in a moment. Today's country market day: I can get smoked meat for two schillings, and at the butcher I have to pay three and a half. Butter is up too."

Maria sighed. There was certainly nothing to oppose to this argument. They certainly had to live thriftily. It was a miracle, anyhow, what Josephine managed to do with the pension money, for it must be confessed that Maria was a gourmet. She had allowed herself to be completely spoilt in the small, choice restaurants of Paris, Petersburg, Madrid, The Hague —everywhere. But Josephine cooked very well. Her baked chickens retained their original tenderness within their crackling dough crusts; her *asperges à la Milanaise* acquired the tang of tomato and melted cheese without forfeiting anything of their delicate aroma, and her *Mehlspeisen* varied *ad infinitum*. If

71

necessary she could bring upon the table a different attractive sweet every day of the year, and so Josephine's appeal to the claims of the kitchen was always the factor that turned the scale in the decisions Maria Ritter still had to take in her seventy-fourth year.

"Yes, yes," said Maria, "I'll get up."

When she was standing in her long pink night-gown on the polar bear-skin, Maria had, as she had every morning, one weak moment. Every morning she was unspeakably annoyed when the moment came for her to undo her nightgown and meet her yellow, heavy and yet withered body under the supple pink washable silk. It was a very difficult and unpleasant moment: but fortunately it did not last long, for she got through it as quickly as possible with her healthy, Viennese optimism. After all, she could still choose with taste the dresses in which she wrapped herself so discreetly, and she had a clever and not very exacting little needlewoman. When she was properly made up, and her hair suitably dressed, she still made a satisfactory impression in a city where a trifle of coquettishness is not begrudged even to older women.

"There now! But I'll read my letters first," said Maria. "You go downstairs meanwhile to that boy. You might tell him I think he plays quite well— only he must exchange his screeching fiddle for a better one. Just have a chat with him and arrange for me to see him soon. But give him the ticket properly in a closed envelope. It's lying on my toilet table."

To the post-war generation, Maria Ritter might seem a made-up, childish, sentimental old woman; but in her heart the red musician's blood still flowed, and it flowed more quickly when touched by musical truth. Maria knew nothing of the young violinist who, hour after hour, had been playing his exercises this last week or two in the little pavilion under her bedroom windows. She only knew that his touch was bold and subtle, his tone full and pleasing. These last days she had often stood by her open window and nodded approval at the virtuosity of his runs up and down the scales. She had surrendered with pleasure to a sweet *cantilena*. Naturally she had asked Hodl his name, and she had succeeded in remembering it, although these days she forgot names so easily. He was called Paul Wolùk. A totally unknown name. But it would not look bad on a bill. . . .

Maria had read through her post, had written just the pleasing, flattering little note to Baroness Märzenburg that the latter would expect in acknowledgment of the snapshot, and had put away in her small satinwood desk the two seats for the first night of *Wozzek* that the management of the Opera had kindly sent her. Josephine should have been back long ago.

But Josephine did not come, and so Maria put on some old kid gloves, took a feather brush, and began to do a little dusting—moving on the dust, Josephine called this method. But it would really have been impossible to disperse the dust in a more thorough fashion from the collection of bibelots and framed portraits that covered the what-nots and side-tables, not only in the sitting-room but into her very bedroom. It was easy for Josephine to say that so far as she was concerned all this might be put away in the cupboard. Maria could not do without this show of tangible souvenirs. Every portrait, every little object had a vital connection with some still sensitive spot in her heart. Every morning Maria with her featherbrush wafted the dust of the years from her memories.

Meanwhile poor Josephine was standing downstairs in Hodl's stacked workshop knocking at the entrance door to the pavilion, but getting no answer. As she stood there, she knew that the peasants of the Naschmarkt were in the habit of returning to their villages at about eleven o'clock. It was an unpleasant situation, and with her thin knuckles she energetically beat the measure of her annoyance on the closed door. Why was there no bell?

Paul Woluk, of course, heard quite well that someone was seeking admittance, but he did not yet feel inclined to get up from his divan. Two white cats lay warm and soft over his feet, a gray one had fallen asleep round his neck, and his eyes were following the movements of a large black tom-cat that, seated on a footstool, was carefully adjusting its tail into the right curl about its paws. 'Let them knock,' thought Paul Woluk as he ran his long white hand over his

74

forehead. 'When it begins to bore them, they'll go away.'

But he had under-rated Josephine's energy, and her thrifty heart that was drawing her to the inexpensive smoked meat in the Naschmarkt. Besides, she had no intention of running down two flights of stairs for nothing. She therefore obtained the victory. When Paul could no longer endure the banging and rattling, he removed the cats from his pyjamas and got up. He opened the door a crack.

"Yes?" he said, "here I am."

"Are you Herr Wolùk?" enquired Josephine. She could see nothing but a hand and a piece of blue striped pyjama sleeve, and was annoyed.

"Probably. My card is on the door," said Paul. Young people these days could be unbelievably rude. Josephine still remembered Maria Ritter's former adorers: there was a great difference.

"Can I come in for a moment?" asked Josephine as politely as she could. Maria would want to know how the young man was living, and what his home was like; besides, she could not have the little chat that had been enjoined upon her through a crack of the door a hand's-breadth wide.

"Geehrtes Fräulein, I'm a gentleman. How could I receive a lady in this attire?" asked Paul. He remembered at the same time that his chamber-pot was still standing in front of the divan. "Just give me your message," he suggested.

To Josephine, pyjamas were no obstacle. She had faded and dried up in the world of opera and ballet, and it took a lot to shock her; but Paul Woluk was a shy, fastidious boy. He would have preferred to die rather than show himself to a stranger with frowsty looks and disheveled hair, even to a tough old servant. So this time Josephine did not get her way.

"Well, what have you to say to me?" insisted Paul. He had already had to tie the tassel of his pyjama trousers more tightly. He was standing with bare feet on the stone floor and was beginning to lose patience.

"I've come from Maria Ritter," said Josephine. She had always been accustomed to finding this name the watchword that opened doors.

"Do I know who Maria Ritter is?" asked Paul irritably.

Josephine's assurance was shivered by the blow— was it possible that in Vienna people did not even know Maria Ritter any longer? But then her whole devoted heart rose up in arms. She pressed her face to the opening of the door, and began to hold forth, relate, celebrate, exaggerate. Paul, on the cold stones, lifted first one foot, then the other. Then, however, the Naschmarkt came back suddenly to her memory again. She delivered her message with the officious good humor of a Father Christmas bringing the children their presents. "Frau Ritter is very interested in your playing. I was to give you this ticket for Thi-

76

baud. Wouldn't you care to look her up some day?"

But by this time Paul Wolùk was at the end of his patience. Why, yes, he would certainly allow himself to be sent like a schoolboy to Thibaud by an interfering diva with hag's teeth! He also pressed his face to the opening and told Josephine several unpleasant things. Then he pushed the door to and went back to his resting-place. The cats miaowed, grateful to have him back, and resumed their places.

A moment later Josephine, disconcerted, was standing beside Maria, who had actually begun to dress by herself. Josephine arrived only just in time to rub down her back. Maria was full of gaiety and insisted upon Josephine's telling her at once everything she had learned of Paul Wolùk.

"I didn't even have a good look at him," said Josephine. "But I saw enough to know that he's an ill-bred, self-opinionated tallow-face."

"Really?" said Maria Ritter. "But you're quite wrong, Josephine. A self-opinionated tallow-face can't play Mozart as he can. I shall have to go to him myself."

"Oh, no, Gnädige Frau," said Josephine, appalled. "On no account must you do that. He really is a lout. When I wanted to give him the ticket he said: 'I belch upon Thibaud, and Maria Ritter can choke.'" The merciful Josephine did not report the worst—that Paul Wolùk had said: "Do I know who Maria Ritter is?"

"Oh," said Maria, smiling, "that makes it really worth while. Undoubtedly there's something in the boy. D'you know what? As soon as I'm dressed, I'll go to him myself."

Maria Ritter had never been married. That would have been superfluous. She had a daughter of five-and-forty whom she had had educated by Franciscan nuns and who was now the bigoted Mother Superior of a small boarding-school for girls at Salzburg. Maria had loved her little daughter very much, but had loved art more, and the worthy sisters had had little difficulty in estranging the child from her too worldly mother.

Maria had had no time to miss her unborn children; but now that she was seventy-four, she missed her grandchildren.

A small, living, rudimentary human being that laughed with a trembling fragrant little mouth. When Maria sat on her chair in the Stadtpark or the Burggarten, among the perambulators and the young mothers, she sometimes longed so fervently to pick up a sleeping infant in her arms, or to run the tip of her finger over a round, soft, little cheek, that she had to get up and move away. It was a wonderful maternal feeling that had blossomed late, and it certainly did not spring from her withered body. It was probably the last flare-up of her fiery love of life. All the youth that was being born into this world was a promise for her own immortality, the immortality of the living, purposeful, turbulent race of men. Everything young was dear to her: the schoolboys and girls who flourished their satchels so nonchalantly as they passed her; the flappers, the students, the builders' apprentices she met on her way; and of course the coming musicians, the young men and girls who smoked their cigarettes outside the coffee-houses round the Conservatoire. Once in every season Maria climbed all the eighty-two steps leading to the fourth gallery at the Opera and sought standing-room for herself behind the balustrade of the promenade among the young people carrying their music scores, merely to warm herself once more at the glow of their whispered discussions. Nobody up there knew her any more. Nobody even wondered who the fat old lady could be who got so troublesomely in the way, while one tried to pay attention at the same time to the conductor, the stage with the soloists, and the score that might at any moment slip off the balustrade; and when at the end of the act Maria descended once more towards the seat in the box that the management had so kindly placed at her disposal, the seat in the box from which the promenade was quite invisible, then she lost herself in thought on the way, and very quietly went past the steps of the upper rows and out of the house by a side door.

"I shall look up the boy before I go out for my walk," said Maria.

Josephine shook her head ironically. "Nothing will come of that," she warned her. "These days they don't want to be pushed and encouraged. They must do everything for themselves. But you can only try. Perhaps he'll treat you better than he did me."

"I expect you tried to play the boss over him. That's not the way to deal with them," said Maria lecturingly. "Just help me with my shoes."

Ten minutes later Maria closed the front door, and Josephine felt to see if it was properly shut. They descended the stairs together, Josephine first in case Maria stumbled. She carried a large string-bag dangling from her arm: she had great expectations of the Naschmarkt.

In the entrance hall, everything was now as gay as could be wished for a golden wedding. There was a marvelous smell of resin, and all the light that the Luftbadgasse was capable of giving streamed in on this June morning through the wide-open doors. Three generations of Hodls were waiting in the entrance hall or on the pavement for the bridal pair, who still tarried in their home, but who would be coming out at any moment to take their places at the head of their descendants in the procession towards the Mariahilf Church. Even a press photographer was there, and Maria, as she surveyed the crowd of those present, was curious to know what he could make of the event. It was neither a handsome nor a noble nor a dignified breed that owed its existence to Hodl and his Resi, and, apart from a few inevitable exceptions, it looked only moderately intelligent. Their appearance revealed the typically Viennese blend of Czech, Hungarian, Polish exoticism with South German stability, in which any truly national character had ceased to be recognizable. Yet they impressed the spectator by their number, their quiet kindliness, and their well-groomed exterior. Of course everyone puts on his best clothes for a golden wedding; but these clothes were after all their very own: Sunday clothes that were hung away during the week, and that helped to distinguish Sundays from working days; decent clothes sewn by Mother herself, none of the trash from a clearance sale that the department stores like to saddle humble folk with. And the curls of the little girls had been duly set in curling-paper, the blouses of the little boys were stiffly ironed.

Of course the few intelligent exceptions turned up their noses at all that. Among the Hodls too, or whatever were the names of the sons-in-law and their children, there were several prophets of the new light who, during the week, wore a minimum of clothing and on Sundays nothing but a bathing-suit. They had come from their settlements or model dwellings to the Luftbadgasse in order to please their parents or grandparents, and were about to accompany the others to church, although otherwise they never went. But little Resi had already nudged one young cousin and whispered to her that she could not go and sit like that in church with her arms bare. She had actually offered her own jumper to cover the fleshly attractions of the other girl. The cousin, however, who was married to a true-blue Young Socialist, was not to be persuaded: in that case she would stay at home and help to get things ready.

And yet she was not really frivolously dressed, this young cousin. She was wearing a snow-white linen frock, attractive white socks with red sandals on her sun-bronzed legs, and a string of bright blue beads round her short-cut blond head. Looked at with an unprejudiced eye, she was more a sight for rejoicing than the other female members of the family, who all wore the gloves and cloak that tradition demanded for a rather solemn churchgoing; and they were prepared reluctantly to admit this too, but they did think all the same that for this once she might have modified her *Naturfreunde* attire. Another cousin was also out of the picture, with her platinum-blond permanent-wave and her wantonly made-up eyes, and she too was looked at askance. There was no getting away from it: the Hodls were averse to excess.

That was why they got on so well with one another. At bottom the Christian Socialist members of the family had very little to say against the reds. As a matter of fact, they were equally proud of the Kinderheime, the Amalienbaden, and the magnificent new technical school, and they were just as keen on getting a flat in one of the great blocks of buildings. If all this were taken away from them, they would have felt themselves unfairly used. But as there was little chance of that, their consciences could safely leave it to their faithful Christian hearts to decide their politics. All the same, even if the family threw up only an occasional Socialist, the majority voted red, although the women in particular rarely missed church on Sunday. Only old Hodl himself, and another stray house-owner here and there, had suffered too much in their pride of ownership to forgive the Sozis their building energies. But of course the family remained the family in all circumstances.

It was really a very united crowd that now looked up in unison, and smiled and pressed forward when Johannes and Resi with their eldest son and daughter and the three grandchildren scattering flowers appeared upon the threshold of their dwelling. All these people belonged to one another, and their place was round their progenitor. Johannes was wearing his top-hat. Oh, it dated from before the war, of course. Who would buy a top-hat these days? But Johannes had made good use of his hat in his time. There were always children to be christened and old relatives to be buried; over and above which a master painter had also his position to consider, even though he did not boast of it. As he stood there, still vigorous, his neat dark overcoat broad over his shoulders, the much used ceremonial top-hat above his friendly red face, and on his arm Mother Resi, small but alive, in decorous black silk and a gold chain, he was a progenitor to be proud of, a promise of health and success to all. Everyone wanted to be first to press his hand; and the small children were lifted over the shoulders of the others so that they could give their grandfather and grandmother a kiss. Johannes nodded and laughed and looked into the faces bending forward: all of them were his close relations. He was enjoying himself to the full; his heart drank in the great day in draughts. Resi's joy was as great, but of another fashion: she had counted all the heads and had seen that only a few were missing. She had seen that each had appeared in his Sunday best, and that the decorations of the entrance hall were jolly good—fir green with a royal display of paper roses and Chinese lanterns. She waved from afar to the oldest workman. "Well done, Franzl!" Her small brown eyes reviewed the multitude, and then suddenly they discovered the photographer—ah, that was a surprise. For Resi, indeed, this was the great, the true, the unexpected surprise of the day, of which she had thought she knew in advance all the surprises; and this surprise—as she understood when the press photographer introduced himself: *Wiener Allgemeine Zeitung*—had been prepared for her by the Young Socialist, who was a compositor there and had warned the editorial staff. At that moment Resi was at peace with the world and with herself—even with the Young Socialist, who was her least beloved grandson-by-marriage.

84

The photographer arranged the bridal pair and their relatives in front of the main gate. He was satisfied. Of all the large families that he had taken in the course of his career, this really was the most characteristically uniform.

From the other side of the street Josephine had been watching with interest, but when the photographer put away his apparatus and the Hodl family proceeded towards the Mariahilf Church in loose formation, she hastened to the Naschmarkt. If she hurried, she could get to Mariahilf before the end of Mass— her shopping-bag was no objection there. She disappeared round the corner of the Luftbadgasse where the smell of garlic from the sausage stores floated in gusts on the warm wind.

All this time, Maria had been standing and waiting at the back of the entrance hall. Not because she was worried about conducting her negotiations with Paul Wolùk in full view of the public, but because the boy himself might feel embarrassed; and so she waited until she had seen the last Hodl depart and until a painter's apprentice who was tuning his mandolin in the workshop had disappeared with his instrument into the Hodls' home. Yes, a small family orchestra was to play today. Mandolins, guitars, and similar instruments, all within their own circle.

Maria was standing in front of the closed door upon which was stuck the befingered visiting-card of Paul Wolùk. She knocked. She knocked and knocked again, waited and knocked once more. But nobody came, and as she was not spurred on by duty or energy as Josephine had been, she looked dubiously at the red knuckle of her index finger and continued to wait. Then, with the roguish little laugh that had accompanied her through life since she had been a young girl, she turned about, stepped across the entrance hall, went out through the back door, and found herself in as dilapidated, neglected a wilderness, overgrown with thistles, as could be found in the heart of the city. It was the backyard of Hodl's house. Before the war it had been let to a maker of gravestones who had fallen on the Isonzo. Among the fragments of granite and freestone still stood many a half-finished cross with its moving traditional inscription— *Meinem vielgeliebten Manne, Ruhe sanft liebe Mutter* —that had never been sold. A weeping angel bending over a broken rosebush still waited for its left wing and a leg. Everything was upside-down, black with dust, brown with moss; and it was even sadder than a church yard because it was completely without significance.

But what was that to Maria? She carried her own good humor with her wherever she went. Cautiously she stepped among the debris and the dirt until she stood before the attractive little baroque door of the pavilion, above which two round Cupids flourished a torch. Maria laughed up at the attractive baby faces, but she could not help sighing too. She knew this entrance, for she had called here last year on an epileptic sculptor whom Hodl had had to have taken to the hospital.

Her hand was on the wrought-iron door knob—a decorative bent tendril; the door gave inwards. 'Of course,' thought Maria. 'Why should a boy like that lock himself in?' She herself was still inclined to leave her doors open. That dated from the time when she had possessed very little worth stealing. She laughed as she shut the door behind her. 'He'll swear when he sees me,' but she was quite sure of herself. Had she not always known how to deal with people?

When, however, she opened the door of the large octagonal room she was after all a little scared by the anxious, angry shout that came to her from the divan. Had she made a mistake after all?

Oh, yes, of course she had made a mistake. It was not at all the same thing when a good-natured old woman came to offer her protection as when a charming singer forced her way into a young artist's room. But how could Maria have learned the difference? She who only that morning had read the "carissima mia" of old Carlo Perrucci?

"But this is an unheard-of impertinence!" Paul Woluk barked at her. "Who asked you to come? You've frightened me out of my life. Didn't I tell that old hag I saw nobody?"

He got up from his divan. He had seized the cover and thrown it round him, and stood there now, thin and ridiculous, between the four frightened cats which spat and stretched their tails in the air. He knew how ridiculous he must look. He noticed too his full chamber-pot and was so ashamed he could have hit her, he could have cried. But with his hands he had to hold the bed-cover round him, and cry he would not. His voice was merely louder and more cutting than usual when he said: "Inspection only upon written application—and now out you go, one, two, three!"

Maria really felt rather sorry. The boy was more nervous than was necessary or desirable, even for a born artist—perhaps it would have been better after all if she had knocked. But it was too late for that now. If she withdrew, everything would be spoilt, and so she came a little further into the room, pushed a pair of shoes on one side with her foot, laid on the floor a pile of music from the one and only arm-chair, and said: "Yes, I'd like to sit down a while!"

Paul Wolùk stood there, stiff and disconcerted, hostile and uneasy. This woman was behaving differently from the way she should have done, differently from what experience had taught him to expect. He had not met with this sort of thing before. He had never yet come into contact with the darlings, even the former darlings, of the public. People who had received their freedom from the public, and upon whom the public no longer imposed its morals or its conventions. Paul Wolùk had only recently come from Graz, where his mother, the doctor's widow, had kept a little boarding-house since his father had failed to return from the Carpathians. In that boarding-house, he had acquired some practice in dealing with compassionate and helpful ladies. He had treated them with tact and caution for the sake of his poor mother, but had nevertheless managed to keep them at arm's length; and now this impertinent old creature had taken him by surprise insufferably, inescapably. In Graz he had pursued his studies in the garage in order to elude praise and criticism in the house, and thus he had been successful in gaining the respect of the few and the cold dislike of the many among the guests. But at least he had been spared their interference in his work—and now this insistent customer was bent upon letting him know that she appreciated his playing, as if that was likely to give him pleasure! 'May you choke, you damned old jade!' he repeated to himself under his breath, and at the same time was helplessly annoyed by his childish, impotent resistance. He did not know what to do. The presence of the stranger jarred heavily upon his jangling nerves. His nostrils opened wide, his hands clenched the bed-cover convulsively. He was suffering acutely from the forced proximity of another human being.

Yet Paul was no inveterate misanthropist. It simply was that he had never so far met anyone to whom he could give his confidence as one equal to another. The only people he had known were the petty middle-class citizens of Graz and, during the last few weeks, his fellow students at the Conservatoire—and these two kinds of people, superficially so different, were equally different from him; both were equally bent upon success and fame. He was not like that. Even his mother shrugged her shoulders with a sigh when she talked about him: he certainly had talent, but he would never get anywhere—his father had been exactly the same: he also had known no ambition.

But his mother was mistaken. It was true that Paul Wolùk did not bother about notoriety and success with people. But he had a gnawing ambition, a consuming pride, an obstinate capacity for perseverance. When he set to work, he toiled like a galley-slave, gave himself no rest, thought of neither eating nor drinking— but only to please himself, to gain his own respect. He was determined he would play—just play—play upon the violin, nothing more. Let others talk about what was fine, what was ugly; he played. But there was hardly anybody who could play, play as the masters themselves heard their music, without thought as to who was listening. And he would repeat forty, fifty times, and the following afternoon another fifty times, the same cadenza, only to put his violin angrily back into its case, and then bring it out again ten minutes later. He was determined to hear himself play this cadenza as it should be played, and if he were not successful on the tenth day, he would be successful on the eleventh. Then, when once he had heard the passage as it really and truly was, he did not play it again for months.

From her armchair, Maria had now seen Paul Woluk as he really and truly was. Ah, yes, Maria had seen many men in her life. She had taken them as they were and never desired to rule or change them. Her happiness consisted precisely in this contact with their ever-changing, living reality. She had sought their innermost tone, listened to it, and felt it within herself, just as Paul Woluk assayed his cadenzas. Maria met this self-centered, proud child, and knew what he was like because there were others like him.

"What a dirty trick of mine, eh?" said Maria. "But I'm like that. If I've a mind to do a thing, then I do it because I can't help myself."

Paul bit his lip. He still had the bed-cover wound firmly round him as he stood there waiting. He would neither speak nor move until this unmanageable intruder was out of the room.

"Of course, you're different," proceeded Maria. "If you don't want to do anything, then you don't do it—am I right? But that amounts to exactly the same thing, my boy."

Paul shuddered—'my boy'—that was the last straw.

"Well, then," said Maria, "you don't want to make my acquaintance. Well, there's no need for you to either. I've known you a long time already. You've got a magnificent left hand, and your touch lacks the

91

merest nothing. You need only work for a year in Paris under Enesco to be as good as Milstein."

'I'd like to see you fall dead!' whispered Paul inaudibly. He could see no way out, and was inexpressibly exasperated at his own impotence: over and above which, the woman was right. His teacher had already told him the same thing—in Vienna they could teach him little more. And then in Paris after a year? Would he not be at a standstill there as he now was here? Going as far as his ability allowed, and yet never coming near to attaining perfection? "God Almighty!" he moaned suddenly, "get on with it, woman!"

"Quiet now," said Maria soothingly. "You need not say anything at all. I understand quite well that I'm annoying you, but that was my intention. You deserve that on account of poor Josephine. *Enfin,* that's another question. She'll make you a liver-paste one of these days all the same. Incidentally, where's your breakfast?"

Paul Wolùk looked involuntarily in the direction of the table; but the cats had already done their worst —the milk jug was empty. Yes, that was to be expected. If he did not prepare his cocoa first thing in the morning, they were before him, the varmints. Maria got up. She noticed the gray puss withdrawing his white milky paw from the jug and licking it with relish. "Heavens!" said she.

"Doesn't matter," muttered Paul. "And may I now

ask you for the last time to mind your own business?"

"Yes," Maria nodded, "that's just what I was intending. I can mind my own business for ten minutes or so—in this armchair with my back turned to you. When you're dressed, we can go on chatting." She rolled the chair towards the window and sank down in it.

'No escape,' thought Paul; but at the same time he allowed the heavy bed-cover to slip from his shoulders with a certain satisfaction.

"What a blessing it is to be a man!" said Maria, conversing over her shoulder. "Just imagine if you were a young girl and I an old gentleman! In that case you'd be compelled to bring the whole house down! Instead of which, see how nicely we're sitting together."

Paul rolled up his pyjamas and slipped on his underclothing. He hurried into his clothes; in a moment, when he had his collar and tie on, he'd show the old bitch the door. He ran a comb through his hair, and slipped on his jacket; but then his eye rested upon the chamber-pot that still stood carelessly in the middle of the room. With the thing in his hand he ran round behind Maria. The only place he could get rid of the contents was on the refuse-heap outside his window, and he tried to empty the pot unseen through the second window.

"Well done!" said Maria, observing his clearing up. "But there's really no need to be embarrassed.

Beethoven had a thing like that standing beside his grand piano when he was at work. You modern people are so depressingly hygienic."

Paul stood still, filled with astonishment, the utensil in his hand. This was something different. Of course, the woman might be odd, but he was not even sure of that. She was certainly not lower middle-class, nor was she a snob. She was original, despite her over-officiousness.

He pushed the chamber-pot under the divan, adjusted the cover, then washed his hands in the basin which, fortunately, he had not emptied the previous day. He opened the window wide.

"A melancholy view," suggested Maria. "But that's not without attraction when one is young, eh?"

Paul Wolùk was now completely dressed and fit to be seen. He could therefore have seized the woman by the shoulders and pushed her outside. He was already standing behind her chair. But suddenly he became aware that his exasperation had evaporated. It had gone, and he did not know how. The fat, peaceful back that Maria turned to him must be the cause, one way or another. He shrugged his shoulders, coughed, and said: "You can turn round again now.—Let me introduce myself. Paul Wolùk."

A nose too long and not straight, a handsome forehead despite somber black hair growing too low, light brown eyes that looked shy when you met them. "Delighted," said Maria. "I'm Frau Ritter, once private singer to a prince. . . . God, do try and be a little friendly—future virtuoso."

Maria noticed that the boy had knit his eyebrows. Magnificent material.

"You sent back my seat for Thibaud. You know best yourself of course. . . ."

"Yes, I do," growled Paul.

"Agreed," said Maria. Self-reliance was the first prerequisite, and actually the boy was right.

"Who would you like to hear then?" enquired Maria.

"Nobody. I want to hear nobody, and nobody need hear me. None of that interests me. . . ." He was silent. He had been on the point of making confidences.

"Exactly," said Maria. "I've occasionally heard that kind of thing before—the artist is his own public. What a despiser of the world you are! But you'll get over that, you know."

Paul was silent. He would have liked to tell her his gospel of life, as on occasion he had done to his fellow-students: to play Bach perfectly and then take veronal. But it seemed impossible to say a thing like that to this old woman who looked about the room with such remarkably alert eyes.

"But where do all these cats come from?" asked Maria suddenly. She counted four, among which was a white one that was obviously in expectation of a happy event. "There'll be ten within a week," she decided.

The boy laughed. It was a rare pleasure to see the shadow slip away from his forehead.

"They lived here before I came. I can't get rid of them," answered Paul. "However, they behave themselves discreetly, they make room when I want to sit down, and don't expect too much affection."

"Oh, yes," said Maria, getting up. "I can make room too, of course, if you want to sit down. And as for affection, I don't expect much of that either at my age. . . ."

That got him. The boy flushed and was about to apologize. Although Maria knew quite well that he had not meant anything unpleasant, she was pleased to see his slight embarrassment. Then, in motherly fashion, she helped him over it.

"And so perhaps I may come back soon and have a chat. But it's a pity you won't let me help you to a ticket or two. You're in Vienna now and you could hear this one and that." She was genuinely sorry she could do nothing for the boy. She would have liked to do a great deal. Then something occurred to her. "Would you like to go to the Opera the day after tomorrow? I've a couple of tickets for *Wozzek*—does that interest you?"

"Are they giving *Wozzek* now, in June?"

"It's festival week, lieber Freund. We have to put our best foot forward for the sake of the Americans. After all, they can't listen to the *Nibelungen* for more than three nights. They've had *Il Seraglio* and *Rosen-*

kavalier already, so now we're producing our latest creation."

Paul hesitated. He would certainly have liked to hear *Wozzek*. He could listen—provided it was not to a violinist. But he could not accept anything—that was the difficulty; and from this woman too, a stranger, whom he had insulted into the bargain. He certainly could not accept anything from her.

"Nonsense, boy," flashed Maria. "In the intervals you can go and stand in the corridor. I can't bear some audiences either, but I hope our visitors will fill the house from top to bottom. The Opera's running at a loss. The entire company has just had to accept a further ten per cent reduction in salaries."

Paul looked shyly towards Maria. She was surely three times as old as he. She was in all probability even nearer death than he—and yet there she stood so firmly rooted in life that he would have been inclined to feel respect just for that—if he had not been compelled to adopt an attitude of slight superiority.

"Well, I'll send you the ticket for *Wozzek* then," said Maria. She smiled a mischievous smile. "But don't be afraid: you won't be saddled with me the whole evening. Of course I must show myself in my seat—but I intend to go and listen upstairs. I want to know what they think of it there."

Paul was about to accept and to thank her. He was seeking for some word that he could say without too much difficulty, but then suddenly they stood riveted,

Maria and he. After their first fright they could not forbear to laugh. From the house droned a wonderful, penetrating noise: it sounded like a swarm of bees gone mad, trying to hold on to a melody. "God Almighty!" said Paul. But Maria realized that it was the mandolins and the guitars that were about to rehearse.

"It's the golden wedding," she said. "Haven't you been invited too?"

Paul had so far only thought of Hodl as landlord, and beyond that had ignored everything connected with the house. Yes, and perhaps that was automatic, whatever one's intellectual standing, when one lived in the back premises. "I don't know these people," said he.

"Oh, but then you must come and have a look," said Maria with a laugh. "We're all dancing together this evening. You don't even need to be invited. Hodl's golden wedding—the Hodls, I mean. The whole street is joining in—something of the soil—you mustn't miss that. I'm going too. Do you know what? I'll come and fetch you."

'No,' thought Paul, 'not that.' The inharmonious whirring and quivering of the guitars was setting his nerves on edge. "I've an engagement," he said decisively and rather surlily. Usually he did not care to speak untruths.

"A pity," declared Maria. "An artist should not let the moment pass." And then she felt she could stay no longer without becoming a nuisance.

OTTO VON WERNIZEK got out at the corner of the Luftbadgasse. True, he had given his address to the taxi-driver at the Westbahnhof: Luftbadgasse 12, but upon reaching the entrance to the street, he had paid the man and sent him away, to the driver's obvious relief. Now he stood there with his large bag beside him and felt himself growing a little melancholy, because the street, even on this radiant June day, seemed much deader and more sunless than he had imagined it during his exile.

'And Aunt Paula lives here with Lili!' he thought. He bore fate no ill-will that since his twentieth year he himself had had to learn to resign himself without protest to such vicissitudes of outward existence as inflation and loss of rank. But he still could not bear to think that his decorative, delicate-minded Aunt Paula, the widow of the charming aristocrat who had represented the Hapsburg monarchy at so many pre-war diplomatic conferences, now had to stagnate in one of those somber old houses lying there in the depths of the Luftbadgasse. 'I'll take her some flowers,' he said to himself, and retraced his steps.

The narrow little shop in the Gumpendorferstrasse was ill-provided. This neighborhood could not permit itself any luxury expenditure. "But why not have artificial flowers? They keep fresh!" advised the garrulous shopkeeper when Otto, finding her lilies too expensive, was unable to make up his mind between the humble roses and the carnations. Only then did he discover that the greater part of the flowers on show were of cotton and paper.

"We couldn't take the risk of having so many living flowers any longer," explained the little woman, "and people almost prefer to buy these imitation flowers nowadays. We have them in pearl and glass too: do you see?"

"Those don't even seem like flowers," said Otto.

"Oh, everyone to his taste: is it not so?—our parish priest won't have them in his church either. But fortunately he'll accept paper flowers—poor people, after all, must have something to take. During May, we sold quite a lot of these artificial white roses for Mariahilf. My husband makes lovely ones. Just see!" and she lifted a bunch of deathly white paper roses.

"No," said Otto, "I can't take those." Suddenly he recalled clearly to mind how his very grown-up cousin Lili used to press her delicate nose voluptuously into a vase of red roses. For a moment he was again the youthful cadet who had offered her flowers with a blush. Of course he had only dared admire her from a distance. Heavens alive!—now she was at least forty, and he was going on for five-and-thirty.

"Just give me the lilies," said he. The little woman hastened to pack the flowers. They were the most expensive bunch in her shop. She bowed him out with a "Küss die Hand, auf Wiedersehen," and opened the door wide for the fine gentleman whom she could not place. From his dress, he might be one of the five thousand Americans who, according to the papers, were holding a congress in Vienna; but his German was too good for that. She looked after him until he turned the corner. A tall, well-built man, and his fair head stood erect upon his shoulders. He had a pleasant way of putting down his feet too. Then she shut the door and sighed. It was not often she had such clients.

Now Otto really did descend the slope of the Luftbadgasse. He did not stand still again. He knew the place once more. Before going to America he had lived with his aunt a year and a half: he had had neither work nor prospects, and she had offered him all she had to offer—a share of the roof above her head. From her poor little pension and the few schillings that Lili's sewing lessons brought in, there was nothing to share. In those days he had repeatedly missed a mid-day meal; but he had never ceased to be grateful to her for the assurance of a place to sleep in. There was nothing of the professional dancer or gigolo about him.

Later he had been able to send her a cheque now and then upon her birthdays, a cheque of limited size, for recently he had had to look after his brother Karl, who was being cared for in what, for the sake of politeness, was called a nerve sanatorium. But all the same he had a hundred-dollar bill in an envelope for her. Of course he could not pay her—he was coming to stay with her. But he could bring a little present with him. Nobody could accept a present more graciously than she. 'Aunt Paula always was an authentic great lady,' thought Otto, 'but she attained perfection only in the Luftbadgasse.' It sounded impossible, but it was a fact. He was looking forward very much to seeing her again.

As he went on, the Luftbadgasse did strike him as being a trifle strange after all. And then he saw the decorations on Hodl's house. 'Heil dem Goldnen Paar?' he said to himself. 'Well, but that must be the Hodls themselves!' And about his mouth there played the open, boyish smile that won men's hearts for him everywhere.

Under the main gate, the mandolin orchestra had already ranged itself, for the Hodls would soon be coming home from church, and they must be greeted with the wedding march. Otto with his bag and his flowers worked his way through the waiting spectators. He nodded and laughed and exchanged greetings in every direction, for he had made many friends during his sojourn in the house. Even Josephine looked after him approvingly as he climbed the stairs towards the upper floors. Poor Josephine! She had missed the tail-end of the festive Mass. She had wasted too much time in a conflict of interests with an unwilling grocer. So now she was waiting to greet the Hodls, her heavy string-bag resting on her hip.

The stairs were very familiar under Otto's feet. Everything was familiar—the oak banisters, smoothed by use, the medallioned window on the first floor, the Yale lock on Herr Friedemann's door, and the antipathy that this Yale lock awakened. Otto had never been well disposed towards Herr Friedemann. He knew what it meant when the small shopkeepers of the neighborhood stood before his door of an evening after closing time. Herr Friedemann still got quite a decent return from the not inconsiderable remains of his war profits by lending small sums against the highest possible rate of interest, and this he did with lower middle-class caution and anxiety over the all-too-palpable risks. As he stood before Herr Friedemann's front door, Otto lived over again the humiliating moment when the fat, puffing money-lender had refused to lend him the travel money for his voyage, against his word of honor and the agate signet-ring of the Wernizek-Bolnanyis. But next moment he laughed at the thought of how the man must be saddened now by his refusal.

'The Kerners still live here too,' Otto observed. This very day he would take the Counselor of Justice the attractive little book of chess problems that he himself had enjoyed so much upon the voyage, and of course he would play chess with him an evening or two. The six days of his newly begun holiday began to assume shape. An evening with Aunt Paula and Lili at the theater, an evening at the Cobenzl—and a few days entirely by himself.

Or perhaps not entirely by himself?

He was standing on the landing of the second floor —yes, the little white enamel plate was still there. Then he registered with astonishment, but with an un-expected deep satisfaction, the shock that the presence of the little name-plate had given him. Did it mean so much—still? Yes—it meant a great deal, still. Some-thing coursed and tingled through his whole frame, to his very finger-tips—it signified warmth and perfume and human intimacy. It signified Rosita Goldös.

'But I must first see Aunt Paula,' he thought, and besides Roserl was of course away at work. 'I might ring her up this afternoon,' he considered further. Suddenly he felt a wonderful unexpected joy that, with the old Vienna, Roserl Goldös also had come close again—Roserl of whom recently he had not thought so very often; and suddenly it was very im-portant too, how she would be after these three years. It was already settled in his mind that he must see her again. But Aunt Paula came first.

When he put down his bag on the third floor, he felt that the steps were high and steep. He stood still a moment and wiped his forehead with his silk hand-kerchief. Then he looked round: someone else had come upstairs just behind him; surely that must be young Jonathan—what a man he had become! He looked cheerily into Daniel's face—and then a new unsatisfying reality thrust away a pleasing memory. Daniel Jonathan was no longer the pretty, dark little boy who made one think of Murillo: Daniel had become a human being, a somewhat melancholy young Jew. Now his eyes reflected the tormenting nostalgia that Wernizek knew in so many Jewish faces, even in America.

"Hallo, Daniel!" said Otto, but it did not sound the same as in the old days.

"Good morning, Herr Graf," said Daniel, and he also used the old greeting without the old tone of voice. Meyer Jonathan had always insisted that the greatest respect should be paid to the impoverished Wernizek family. Meyer Jonathan was aware of the dignity of a hierarchy. He had vigorously enforced the "Herr Graf" upon Daniel; but now Daniel listened acutely to his own words.

"Oh, come," said Otto, "let's drop the title—I got rid of it in America. Tell me, how are you and your grandfather getting along?"

Daniel could find nothing to say but a perfunctory: "Quite well, thank you." That would be the quickest way of releasing himself from the other. The distance between this man and himself had become too great— especially after the night he had spent. What had he in common with this imposing though friendly person,

105

whose roots were planted in such a different soil? Daniel was already too old and still too young to surrender to the simple human attractions he experienced. The distinctions his now active mind drew shut him off ruthlessly from the man opposite him. Besides which, he was now, after all that had happened, much too empty, too exhausted, and too bewildered to want further contact with anyone.

"I'll come and look your grandfather up," said Otto. He had abandoned his familiarity. He accepted the fact that Daniel was grown up. He turned to his aunt's front door and rang. Staring vacantly at the wrought-iron ornaments of the door, at the broad but unpolished name-plate, at the little bottle of milk that stood near the door-post, he listened, and when he heard nobody he rang a second time.

Meanwhile Daniel had gone in. He asked a question; and a woman's voice replied. Then suddenly a queer feeling came over Otto as he stood there on the dusty landing between the two closed doors, and he noted with great disappointment that now he was here he felt none of the joy on his homecoming that he had promised himself during his journey.

But then a wave of sound came up the stairs: the band had struck up the festive march. There was shouting and singing and cries of "Hoch, hoch!" Good-humored, lower middle-class revelry resounded through the house. Otto had to laugh in spite of himself. Then he laid his ear against the keyhole and rang for the third time.

He put down the lilies on his bag, and rang at the Jonathans'. The charwoman looked him up and down before she answered his question. Yes, the family was certainly at home, and so far as she knew there was no sickness. But it often happened that people stood there ringing in the morning and nobody opened the door. Usually she did not see the young lady until about two o'clock, when she took in the milk. The gentleman would be well advised to come back about that time.

Of course he could leave his bag at the Jonathans'.

"Would you mind keeping the flowers too for the time being?" asked Otto, and the charwoman willingly took the sheaf of lilies under her protection. Then Otto stood once more between the two closed doors on the empty landing with the little bottle of milk. And now there was only one direction: the staircase that led below and out of the house.

FRÄULEIN GOLDÖS had made up the cash and was bending over the assistant who was taking her place. Her pencil ran down the columns of figures. She looked at her watch and wrote at the bottom of the sheet: "Taken over by Erna Lanz, 12.35"—then they both put their initials.

"Enjoy your lunch," said the assistant. She belonged to the second lunch period. Well, of course, obviously the head cashier chose the best time for her meal.

Roserl Goldös was hungry. She had the pleasurable feeling that she would enjoy her mid-day meal. As she descended the broad middle staircase, she considered what she should have. Goulash?—No, it was too hot for that. Asparagus with eggs?—Perhaps. But that was not substantial enough when one had one's evening meal only at seven o'clock. Cutlet with roast potatoes?—That was more suitable. Roserl Goldös found it worth while to render account to herself of what the daily meal did for her. She was healthy, and intended to enjoy everything that her active existence had to offer her in the way of good things.

It had a great deal to offer, and Roserl rejected

nothing. Dignified, tasteful clothes, well-fitting shoes, properly prepared meals, an expensive but clever and hygienic coiffure, and now and again a pleasant week-end in some good hotel, either with or without a cheerful companion. Roserl Goldös was not frivolous, really not! Would a frivolous woman have gone far enough to be head cashier at Korngross's? She was simply frank, a socially independent, healthy, pretty woman of six-and-twenty with a good heart, a sense of humor, and a dislike of affectation.

At Korngross's she was appreciated by everyone, of what ever standing. Especially for her sake, Herr Korngross came occasionally to the chief cash-desk, although for the rest he had resigned all supervision to the present management; and the packers wrapped her purchases more carefully and generously in tissue paper than they did for any client; and when she stood in the lift, the lift-boy's pale face brightened, and he actually noticed once more past which landing he was gliding. Roserl Goldös lavished her gesticulations and her powerful handshake. Everyone at Korngross's looked up when she passed by.

Roserl was very attached to Korngross's too. These days, she had no other interest that could compare with Korngross's. She knew every department of it, the people and the things. She was as quick as the supervisors to see when the earthenware department failed to keep up-to-date, or when the ladies' ready-made clothes department was over-stocked. She took the trouble to look about in the business, not as an inquisitive employee but as a fellow worker satisfied by her daily activities. She could quite well imagine devoting her whole life to the success of the Korngross Department Stores.

She reached the last turning of the staircase and glanced over the ground-floor departments. She was not particularly pleased with the amount of custom. Just half-past twelve—where were the shop assistants and clerks of the neighborhood who dropped in to make their purchases before going home for their meal? It was much too empty. The few Americans choosing presents in the central hall did not compensate for that.

"I see too much floor," she said to the reception clerk who stood beside her looking down. "Has it been like that the whole morning?"

"The whole morning," the young man assured her, "and yesterday it was the same."

Fräulein Goldös knit her eyebrows. Slowly her eyes wandered over the tidy counters, the untouched piles of smooth artificial silk, the gaping saleswoman in the handkerchief stand. But then the dissatisfied furrow between her eyes disappeared again—something indefinable there below brought a little smile to the corner of her mouth. She herself was unaware that she smiled—it just happened, as a child laughs in his sleep.

She descended a few more stairs. From there she

could see more clearly the woolens department, and behind that the umbrellas and gloves. In the ties department, right at the end, stood someone in a gray suit looking through a tray of oddments. The smile around her right nostril grew deeper. Her eyes hung on a lock of hair like ripe corn. 'The exact color,' she thought. Then she shrugged her shoulders. Many lands and seas lay between Otto von Wernizek and Korngross's.

'I'll go and eat at the Goldene Pfau,' she decided. 'I want to hear some music.' Rosita Goldös was not as a rule keen upon a musical accompaniment to her mid-day meal. But for every woman there sometimes comes a moment when she wants to glide on the rhythm of a melody. 'And in that case I'll have asparagus after all,' she decided, as the porter turned the revolving door for her.

But next moment a breath-taking, powerful, moving terror obliterated all thought in her. She put her hand to her heart, her handbag fell at her feet. "God, it *is* you," she whispered.

Otto was standing beside her. He picked up her handbag and absent-mindedly slipped it under her arm while she remained looking at him as if a miracle had happened before her wide-open eyes. But when he took her hand and bent over it with that airy, courtly, yet charming gesture that the youngest Vienna has now lost, she began to realize that he was

111

back, he himself, back in Vienna, back in the world—perhaps back in her life.

Back—then it had been he after all there among the ties. And she smiled. Of course she ought to have known—there was no other man who could have reminded her of him.

And now these two human beings were standing next to one another, perfectly quiet and motionless, but perfectly and tensely alive. It was a wonderful moment, a coming together more wonderful than any physical coming together between this man and woman had ever been or could be again—yes, it was a happiness-bringing conquest over everything physical. At that moment, for each of them the other appeared radiant with dear memories and with a long-awaited promise—it was a pregnant moment that overflowed all frontiers. They stood within the moment, and each felt the other's presence; beyond there was nothing.

The commissionaire held back the revolving door and stared discreetly through the plate-glass window into the Mariahilferstrasse. He took part in what he knew was happening behind his back. The commissionaire was a judge of men, as it was his business to be.

When he heard a movement behind him, he gave the revolving door another little push. Then he nodded approvingly once or twice as he looked after them. Fräulein Goldös had chosen for herself an up-standing young man.

Otto and Roserl walked along the broad basalt pavement of the Mariahilferstrasse. They had passed many broad window-panes before they needed to say anything. That had been the astonishing thing about their earlier relationship, this silent understanding of each other's being which had given one direction to their bodies and their thoughts. Oh, their thoughts were not roaming far. They were making no extraordinary discoveries, they were not really exceptional people, Otto von Wernizek and Rosita Goldös, and that was why the first thing Otto said was: "Where shall we go?" and Roserl knew already: "Not to the Goldene Pfau: there's music there. Let's cross over to Zum Auge Gottes. Perhaps there's still room in the garden."

"Right," replied Otto, and then they looked at each other and laughed.

Of course there was nothing to laugh about, but when they were together they understood one another primarily through their laughter. Even when Otto found himself thinking of Roserl in Midland, he felt his worries evaporate in what as a boy he used to call "an inner chuckle." Roserl herself laughed easily and naturally, but not loudly, as do nervous, unbalanced women who laugh too much. She laughed with her eyes, and with the upturned corners of her small upper lip; but the surest sign of her pleasure and delight was the appearance of a little dimple in her left cheek.

Otto had seen this little dimple in her soft round cheek by the time he sat opposite her at table. He admired it. He lost himself in it, until he felt a tiny pressure against his knee, and then he saw the little dimple appear in her right cheek. The whole of Roserl was laughing, and he noticed that the waiter standing by them was amused too.

"What are you having?" asked Otto.

"Cutlet with roast potatoes."

"And I'll have a *Bauernschmaus*," said Otto. It was rather mad to eat sauerkraut with bacon on a warm day in June; but for three whole years he had seen no *Bauernschmaus*.

"Then I'll have *Bauernschmaus* too," ordered Roserl.

"A family dinner again," said Otto, beaming, and Roserl laughed in response. A family dinner—that was what they used to call the menus they composed together after joint consideration upon their week-end expeditions. Not expensive courses, in view of Otto's lack of income, but it would have been unsociable not to eat the same thing.

"What a pity I didn't think of it before; then I could have ordered a cutlet too," said Otto in self-reproach. "Do you think it dreadful to eat *Bauernschmaus?*"

And then Otto saw something glow in Roserl's eyes

that was not there in the old days, in the good, old, light-hearted days.

"Not with you," she said, and there was no sentimentality in that reply.

The waiter had removed the still half-filled dishes of sauerkraut. *"Bauernschmaus* is more attractive from a distance than at close quarters," said Otto. "Exactly the opposite of you, Rosamündchen." He heard himself say it. It sounded ordinary, and yet it would not have seemed too bad once upon a time. Perhaps the Roserl who sat opposite him now was no longer quite the Roserl of old—certainly she was no longer quite the jolly girl always ready for a joke. She was older, perhaps also wiser. 'And finer,' he thought to himself. 'I should not dare to take the same liberties with her as in the old days.' He could not help laughing as he thought of their first kiss behind Father Hodl's painted cupboards. But then he asked gravely: "May I still say Rosamündchen, little one?"

He was disappointed that he had to repeat the question; but then Roserl answered: "Oh, yes."

"Has nobody called you that since?" pursued Otto.

"No one else has been allowed to call me that," said Roserl, but she did not look up and into his eyes, as he had hopefully expected. Something that must be very serious made her press her lips together. Now nothing about her laughed.

115

"We'll order some fruit," said Otto, looking round for the waiter. "Strawberries."

The waiter served them, choice and on ice, and accompanied by a crystal sugar-sifter. Strawberries in June are actually a very ordinary phenomenon, but a good restaurant proprietor can make a distinguished-looking dish of them all the same, especially to the order of an apparently well-to-do German-American. The waiter went so far as to take a little vase of roses from the nearest table and with a friendly smile placed it beside the lady's finger-bowl.

"I've only time for a cigarette," said Roserl.

Otto had already laid his case upon the table. He watched Roserl's brown, well-tended hands choose a cigarette and light it. 'I should have given her a light,' he thought; but that was no serious matter. Roserl knew perfectly well how to help herself without fuss. Her hand with the shiny pink nails, her round firm arms with the shiny golden wristband, moved up and down as she enjoyed her cigarette—his gaze accompanied and found rest in her calm movements.

The warm air was redolent of strawberries. From a window came the soft wail of an infant accompanied by the soothing voice of the mother. Above them on the roof a blackbird whistled. In the small restaurant garden the feet of the waiters crunched the gravel, discreetly. Otto leant over the table.

"And how many friends have sat with you like this since I was here?" And again he heard himself

116

say this as though he were palliating something—a little masterfully, as to a child whom one would not think of punishing for his offense.

On Roserl's forehead there was now a deep furrow that Otto had never seen before. She shrugged her shoulders and slowly blew the smoke through her nose. Her nostrils were very pale—almost transparent. Otto noticed that his hands were growing moist. He suddenly felt very gauche as he sat there —an extraordinarily disconcerting experience in Roserl's presence. Everything in this recovered world was different from what he had expected. No, this was no longer the little friend who had so carelessly given him her youth. This was something new and unknown. He leaned back in his chair and saw her sitting there erect, her comely dark head perfectly poised upon her straight neck. This was a lady— and not quite that either: it was a young, conscious woman, a handsome woman with bearing.

"Don't be angry," he said hastily. "Of course I ought not to have asked that."

"But I'm quite prepared to reply." Roserl bent forward and carefully pressed the glow of her cigarette-stump to death in the ash. "Yes, friends have sat with me here and at a number of other places. I'm not a nun—you might have known that. Why did you come back when you might have known that?"

Her arm with its outstretched questioning hand lay straight in front of him on the table. With strange clarity Otto saw each downy hair and the pale blue streak down the mat skin of her forearm. His hand fastened upon her hand. His fingers enclosed her wrist. "Because I longed for you," he said.

Roserl shook her head. "You didn't even write to me, not once in three years. True, you've come back. But not for me." She looked over his head into space —roofs, roofs, houses, the red striped linen of a sunshade. Then she said: "I thought I had ceased to long for you."

Greedily he leaned forward. "Then you did long, Rosamündchen?"

She continued, speaking into space as if answering herself. "In three years not a single letter. True, you did say: 'I won't write, I won't hold on to you'—but you should have done it all the same. If you had longed, you would have written."

'It's true, perhaps it's true,' thought Otto— 'For her, just for her, I didn't long so terribly. It wasn't so difficult for me to abide by my decision not to trouble her with my letters. But for everything together, the old country and Aunt Paula and St. Stephen's and poor old Karl and the gray mist above the Hermannskogel; and also for her, for her mouth, her mouth and her whole warm soft skin, for all that I longed until it hurt—

'And for all that I shall long again when I'm back in Midland,' he realized suddenly. 'I ought not to have come to Vienna for six days, like all the others.

118

I did not need to come in order to see Vienna. When I close my eyes every little spot of the town is before me, and six days to live with the city and the people —that's much too short.'

Roserl's hand was still lying quiet and motionless under his. He looked at her. The furrow had disappeared from her forehead. She saw that he was emerging again from his thoughts, and she nodded to him with an understanding little laugh. Then suddenly it became clear to him what it was that was changed in her, why she could no longer be the gay child of former years. She had passed through a great sorrow—and through her struggle against sorrow.

His whole warm simple heart went out to her. Everything was driving him towards her—consciousness of guilt, the fact that he was a little flattered, as men are, and especially a pure, boyish compassion for all suffering creatures, a compassion for others that had remained with him since childhood. All the profound, hidden tenderness that had lain fallow over there, that had found no outlet, even in his thoughts, flowed towards her.

"I was not aware that I longed for you," he said humbly. "I longed for everything here, for everything equally badly. You can't understand it if you haven't been through it yourself. Everything over there, every human being, every object is different from here. Until at last you cease to know exactly of

what and whom you are thinking, when that longing
for home comes over you. You only know that life is
miserable and not worth living—and that everything would be all right if you could ski once more
on the Semmering."

"Poor boy!" said Roserl. Her mouth had grown
tender. Otto noticed, and was astonished that it could
make him so happy. He bent further forward, until
he could look up into her eyes.

"But you knew that you longed for me, Rosamündchen?"

He wanted her answer. Oh, he did not want any
confessions. He understood perfectly well that she
had not waited for him like Solveig in that tedious
song. But he wanted to know whether he had a right
to her company, whether he was not an intruder. He
wanted her to say what he was to her, here and now.
He did not want a little bit of love for auld lang
syne. He had quite forgotten the mood in which he
had waited for her awhile back at Korngross's, count-
ing upon a continuance of their happy, care-free relationship, even though it were only for the six days
of his holiday. Everything was different from what
he had expected. He himself was different, the woman
was different, and he wanted this different woman to
love him. He kept his eyes upon hers. He was determined to get a reply.

And then her eyes wandered from the fair lock of
hair that had been the first thing she had recognized

to meet his eyes. Rosita Goldös had honest eyes—
she had always had them; but now those eyes radiated
the higher integrity of the feeling, knowing, ripe
woman who allows herself to answer that her whole
being is prepared to give. Her glance sunk away into
his, and again there flowed around them a radiant,
undivided moment.

Her hand trembled under his. Otto saw that her
eyelids drooped listlessly. "You must come away with
me now," he said. "We must go somewhere together,
out into the country."

But then with an unexpected quick movement that
shook him fiercely and frightened him, she withdrew
her hand. "No," she said decisively. "I must get back
to work." She got up, and was at once the practical,
energetic Fräulein Goldös to whom the Korngross
directors were thinking of giving the power to sign.
She pressed her little red hat into place behind her
right ear, dabbed some powder on her nose, and
beckoned to the waiter.

"No, no, Roserl, it's not like that now—of course
I pay," said Otto. "And you can't run away like this
either. You can't leave me to sit here alone." He
broke off: she had said those last words, the very
same words, one evening three years ago.

"Why didn't I take you away with me to Midland,
Rosamündchen?" he said pensively, addressing the
question to himself, not to her.

She did not answer. She had already slipped on

121

her gloves; but she waved the waiter away. Then she picked up her bag and smiled at him, wise and motherly. She ran her gloved hand over his hair.

"Half-past one, boy," she said. "Korngross's doesn't approve of late-comers. It was nice of you to come and see me." And then she bent down. Her mouth lay on his forehead.

His hand seized hers, but she was already going. "I'll ring you up this afternoon," he called after her, and then he sat in front of the silver fruit-dish with the little mountain of cooled strawberries—alone and deeply bewildered.

'Why didn't I take her with me at the time?' he asked himself. But that did not seem to be the right question. It was obvious that he could not have taken her away with him to an uncertain future. Could a man detach a girl from all security without giving her something in return? When in the old days a Wernizek had loved a woman he could not marry, he had been in a position to make her life full and rich, even outside legal marriage. But what could he have done for Roserl in America? Left her alone the live-long day in a bare boarding-house room while he worked at some little clerical job from which he might get a week's notice? Besides which, he had not even had money to pay for her passage. Madness!

'But why didn't I stay here?' With a deep sigh he felt that that was the real point. It now seemed impossible that he could have abandoned all this so carelessly for three years—the city, where every building, the trams, the trees, the advertisements, even the very trucks looked at him with their own unchangeable physiognomy—the people, who spoke his own tongue—and the girl, who had loved him so simply and bravely in all his poverty.

Of course he knew very well why he had not stayed. He could easily go over all the arguments again on his fingers: no food, no clothes, not a single hope— and over there, the offer of a decently-paid job of work. Secretary to the director of a well-known orchestra: the very job for a man who had been educated at a cadet school and knew nothing useful except perfect French, German, and English, and happened also to know something about music. 'Could a Wernizek-Bolnanyi become a street cleaner in Vienna?' muttered Otto to himself; and then suddenly he knew the unexpected answer to that question. 'Why not?' was the answer, and that brought Otto right up against his aristocratic pride.

Now, after three years in America, he had to admit it: 'Damn it all, it would have been better if I had swept the streets in Vienna. What does a Wernizek mean in Midland? I ought to have got over all that —then I should be standing now upon a streetcar on the Ring or directing the traffic on the Scheeden-brücke.' He sighed. 'But perhaps it was just for Aunt Paula's sake that I didn't do it.'

There lay the true answer before him, very clearly. Yes, of course, he had not done it because of Aunt Paula, because of what it would have meant to Aunt Paula if he, the last remaining Wernizek sound in body and mind, were to earn his bread with his hands like any proletarian. But it was not because of that alone: it was also because he himself in his heart of hearts, where will and reason have no say, continued, in spite of everything, to feel exactly as she did—that it was something shameful. Something shameful that the delicate sensibilities of which he was the bearer—sensibilities cultivated through the centuries—should be lost in the coarse rhythm of physical labor. Was that aristocratic pride? Well, and if it was, it was at the same time consciousness of one's own high value; and that Aunt Paula had understood better than he at the time, when she forbade him to inscribe himself at a labor exchange.

With a jerk, he sat up straight. He was aware once more of the time and the place. Yes, it was after all worth traveling to Vienna for six days in order to meet Aunt Paula. He had intended to go to her at two o'clock. How could he have forgotten? Just imagine: suppose Roserl had gone into the country with him, then he would have kept Aunt Paula needlessly waiting a whole day. It was incomprehensible that she should have slipped his mind. Of course she came first. There was nothing finer and nobler in the world than she.

He buttoned up his coat. He noticed the strawberries in front of him and began to eat. He enjoyed them one by one. He looked up past the backs of the houses, towards the blue sky above. The delicate scent of lime flowers drifted over the roofs and sank into the garden, where it blended with the pleasant culinary smells from hot dishes and the little clouds of stimulating cigarette smoke that came floating past on waves of sun-warmed air. He smiled. 'As a street cleaner, I certainly shouldn't have sat here either.' He ceased to question. Life was much too difficult, too insoluble; one asked questions, but one was never satisfied with the answers.

He looked at his watch: a quarter to two. He would pay, and go to the Luftbadgasse.

As Otto walked through the streets, he looked about him. Everything was good and familiar. The city took him to her arms like a fond mother her small boy. She directed his attention: Do you see this? Do you see that? And everything was as it should be, even though it was perhaps a little inadequate after America. He hurried over the uneven cobbles; and it was a pleasure to feel them through the soles of his shoes. He smiled at the young girls on their way to work with cheap flowers in their little hats. He even found pleasure in the clumsy make-up of their painted faces. He was grateful to them for being different from the American women he knew: who were nothing more than a skin, a fine, smooth, well-cared-for skin around a strange jumble of superstition, sensuality, and egoism. Here walked these children who were like the old Roserl—round, warm, living children of the people, without perversities.

And then he was before the Apollo Theatre and descending the four-and-thirty steps towards the Luftbadgasse.

The Luftbadgasse was still at its mid-day meal. The children were all indoors. Only the pigeons pattered on their coral-red feet in the middle of the street and pecked fussily in the refuse. The luxuriant blue and green of their radiant breasts moved up and down under the steel-gray feathers of their wings. Otto stood still and looked at the mobile little creatures. It was as if he saw for the first time what a pigeon really looked like. He stopped there until the whole flight, one after the other, was driven flapping on high. Then he went on, happy.

The Hodls also were at their mid-day meal. From the living-room resounded the loud, bustling clatter of eating-utensils and chattering, laughing voices. In the entrance hall, an apprentice was drawing jugs full of foaming beer from a dark, moist barrel, and as he stood beside him, Otto felt how cool this beer must be. He would have liked to stay and watch longer; but the boy turned the tap off and carried his jugs inside.

Upstairs at the Jonathans' the charwoman opened the door to him. "I've handed in your things next door already," she said, and was astonished that Otto did not look more grateful. He certainly thanked her, but feebly, and as she went in again she shrugged her shoulders. But she could not know that Otto had been picturing Aunt Paula taking the sheaf of white lilies from his hands.

He rang the bell, and though it was some while before he heard anyone approach, he did not ring a second time. Within, subdued footsteps were moving about, and the floor cracked now and again. Otto thought of thick, black felt shoes: that was how the night nurse had walked about after his operation for appendicitis. Then, unexpectedly, the front door was opened. In the doorway stood a bent, drab little woman on flat knitted slippers. Aunt Paula: was this Aunt Paula?

'No'—something in Otto rose up in protest—'no —of course not—no, it can't be—it mustn't be—it's simply impossible.' But at the same time he observed that Aunt Paula's white hair was screwed up into a thin, untidy knot in the middle of her small old woman's head, and that her poor, pale, dandruffed skull was visible everywhere through the scanty hairs. It was the first thing he noticed, and he could not help seeing it, for Aunt Paula was standing there with bent head before him. She did not look up. Her arms hung limp beside her spotted black skirt. 'Is she ashamed?' wondered Otto, feeling himself far too healthy and large and well-dressed. But then she held out a thin, small, limp, yellow hand with long black nails; and when Otto took that passive, slender hand between his, he found nothing there at all, no shame, no joy at his coming, no emotion whatever. It hurt him. There was a black hollow in his heart from which the pain swelled and spread. And then he pushed the pale little woman inside. He closed the door, and pressed her to him. With his large warm hands he caressed her small bony head. He wanted her to say something, to cry, to laugh. He wanted her to put her arms about him. But he pressed to himself nothing except an inert, dried-up little body that had ceased to react. He let go of her. "Where's Lili, Aunt Paula?"

She pointed to the bedroom. "Lili is busy dressing."

He followed her into the dining-room. His bag lay there already. The lilies lay next to it upon the floor. He picked them up and put them on the table; then he looked round. It was semi-dark and that was strange at mid-day in June, even in the Luftbadgasse; but he saw why—the Venetian blinds had not been drawn up, and the double windows were closed. A sickly atmosphere of musty fabrics, old wood, and the pitiable exhalations of an old woman's unwashed clothes hung in the room. It was not sweltering there on this hot day—only musty, stiflingly musty. The room was musty to the point of suffocation.

"May I open the window?" He could not help it. He had to say it. The atmosphere was not to be borne. The old woman was silent. She had sagged down by

128

the table. Nothing about her stirred. Otto pushed open a window, and drew up the blinds. Then he turned round. He had to force himself to look at her.

The first thought that crossed his mind was: Morphine! But that was impossible. She could not afford that. And yet her whole withered, shriveled appearance pointed to some narcotic. What could it be? What could have ruined her so?

Against the wall behind her, in its broad, gilded frame, hung the imposing portrait by Lenbach of his deceased uncle, Count Felix von Wernizek-Bolnanyi. So that had not been sold yet; and the miniatures were still there too. No, it was not morphine —but what was it? On a mirror-console stood the heavy onyx bowl with the massive gold foot—a present from the Emperor Francis Joseph to his representative at the Treaty of London, and for the first time it occurred to Otto that this was insane, that that bowl ought to have been sold long ago. But at any rate he was sure it was not morphine.

"How is everything here?" he asked at last, forcing his voice to a tone of brightness.

"Well, very well," said the old woman, nodding her head gently. It continued to nod, ten, twelve times, then it stood still.

Otto felt grief thick in his throat: her voice was so unrecognizably thin and broken. He could say nothing more. He would wait till Lili came. He waited. He had learnt patience with Mr. Haymaker. It was

129

certainly not easy to be patient, to wait, when one came of a race that, from father to son, had learnt that a man must assert himself—chivalrously, but conclusively. On the other hand, of the race of Wernizek-Bolnanyi were also born religious gentlemen who celebrated long masses, and devout monks who spent a lifetime bowed in humility under the rules of some order.

Otto had learned to wait. As he waited, he looked about him and recognized the room. He recognized it, and did not recognize it. Cobwebs hung from the ceiling and between the furniture. A curtain had slipped hopelessly away from its rings, a torn footstool supported a rickety sideboard. Things had not been like that when he went away. Of course, these women had not run the house like trained servants—he himself could see that they handled their dusters amateurishly. That distressing North German tidiness that one could almost smell in the houses of lower middle-class families had never reigned here. But that was just what was so wonderful about Aunt Paula: everything round about her had always retained its being and its shape. The Macquart bouquets —genuine ones, arranged by Macquart himself—had kept their useless grace of waving grasses and feathers, and the Gobelin upholstery on her chairs had been fresh and unsullied as though its wonderful tints came from an imperishable world.

Now the Macquart grasses hung down broken, the

130

green parrot feathers were speckled with fly spots. And on the cover of his chair was a large gray fat stain. The top of the rosewood table was covered with deep-bitten circles. He ran his hand over the damaged varnish. Then he looked up quickly.

"Aren't you going to eat?" he asked. Only now did it strike him that the table was not laid, nor were there any traces of a meal that had been consumed. "Haven't you eaten?" he repeated, articulating clearly as though he were speaking to a deaf person. She shook her head and said nothing. It seemed to cost her too great an effort to move her lips. She tried her best, but no words came. It was quiet in the room, terrifyingly quiet; and then Otto noticed that the clock did not tick. He glanced at the large white marble timepiece where Cupid and Psyche stood petrified in an embrace; the hands hung limply downwards. Time stood still.

And now he too continued to wait outside time. The sounds that came in through the open window lost all significance in that room. They were rather troublesome, that was all. The little old woman opposite him did not even appear to hear them. She looked down at her limp, lifeless hands that she had laid in front of her on the table. From time to time she nodded her head sideways, as though she were about to fall asleep.

Otto could not avert his eyes from her. His brain inexorably registered each of her pottering move-

131

ments, each little nasal sound that came from her. A feeling of dull helplessness seized him. There was no question of saving her. Nothing he could do to help. What he saw was beyond help. He no longer sought the cause. His own thoughts grew dim. Only now did he feel the effects of the long journey he had behind him. His cheeks stretched themselves in an irresistible desire to yawn.

But then a motor horn blared in the street.

Otto jumped up. He shook himself like a wet dog. He could not bear to go on waiting like that—nobody could have borne it. "I'll just go and see Lili," he said. His aunt made no movement. Three years ago he would never have thought of seeking his cousin Lili in her bedroom. Now he thrust open the door as though to let air into a room where somebody lay fainting.

But Lili had not fainted. With pattering, hasty steps she was moving backwards and forwards between her toilet table and the cupboard. In her agitated activity she seemed to have dragged all her belongings out of the cupboard, and was now rummaging in a disorderly heap of clothes. On the table lay curling-tongs smoking in the spirit lamp. A broken staylace dangled smoldering next it: Otto extinguished the glowing end between his fingers. Only then did he notice the pitiable little smile with which Lili welcomed him.

No, Lili was not apathetic like her mother—rather

the opposite. Two bright red spots shone on her thin cheeks. She pressed his hands, she rolled a small arm-chair from a corner and insisted that he should sit down. She ran from one corner of the room to another as though she were searching for something; but there was nothing she sought. Her hands held a faded dressing-gown drawn tightly across her breast, and every time she passed Otto she gave a poor, distorted little laugh that brought tears to his eyes.

"Well, Lili?" said he.

There it was again; he could not bear to see it.

"But what's the matter with you two?" he asked. "You must tell me what has happened. After all, I'm the only one left now whose business it is," he added. It sounded hard, and then he knew suddenly that it was true.

Lili had possessed a remarkably pure, straight profile. He remembered it, now that he saw her sideways as she bent over the toilet table. But in these three years, all the lines of her face had become uncertain, as though a shaking hand had made a tracing of a noble outline. Her mouth, her cheeks, trembled. 'Ah,' thought Otto, 'she's an old woman too, already— worse, an old maid.' He went up to her, and put his arm about her shoulders: he had never dared do that before. She had been too long his beautiful cousin. He caressed her shoulder gently, like a brother. "Just tell me," he insisted, "just tell me."

She sobbed, a short sharp sob, and leant her head

against his arm. "There's nothing special," she whispered against his arm. It was a strange whisper, the words ran into one another. It was difficult to understand her.

"But there is something special," said Otto positively. "Your mother's ill—anyone can see that, and your flat is simply unrecognizable. Something has happened here, and I insist upon knowing."

She was about to speak. She swallowed and breathed more quickly, and then her lips parted. She spoke rapidly, in a high-pitched nervous voice; and at her first words Otto knew why she had so long kept up that convulsive, nervous little laugh of hers with mouth closed: she had not dared to speak—she was ashamed to. Because she no longer had any teeth.

He bent his head over her pitiably curled, discolored locks. He listened and tried to understand. It was not easy, but he managed to discover what she wanted to tell him. She panted and whispered and crooned the words that had been shut up within her all this time. She did not hear what she was saying. For the moment, she was unconscious that her toothless mouth was misshaping every word. She spoke and went on speaking to herself, took a deep breath and spoke again.

"Oh, it's easy for you—'Just tell me, just tell me' —you can talk; but if I try to talk, everybody looks at me, and I can be thankful if they're good enough not to laugh in my face. Everywhere they've laughed

134

at me—at the butcher's, at the baker's, the women in the Naschmarkt—wherever I went. I had to send away my pupils one after the other: the children sat grinning and looking at my mouth. I couldn't let that go on, could I?"

"No, no," said Otto, patting her back gently and consolingly. "Of course you couldn't. But didn't you need the money for those lessons?"

"Need it? It was indispensable! You know that. But all the same I couldn't allow myself to be ill-used by those little serpents, and mamma said so too. 'Send them away,' she said. She was glad when they stopped coming. Then we didn't have to clean the flat any more. That saved a lot of trouble. Everything could be left just as it was. And now we don't even need the money."

"You don't need it?"

"No, we don't. What was that money for? To eat, wasn't it? Simply so that we could eat. The pension covered the rent. But why need we eat? Surely just to keep alive. And had I to allow myself to be plagued hour after hour by those naughty children simply so that we could go on living our little bits of lives? So we decided we must just eat less."

"But that's impossible. You couldn't eat less."

"Oh, yes," whispered Lili, and nodded, a determined, persuasive, fatuous little nod. "You don't need to eat much just to keep alive. It's wrong to take one's life, of course. But it's not wrong to say: 'Thank you,

I make no use of my life. I withdraw myself a little.'
And it goes quite easily, really, once you've got into
the way of it."

Otto listened with the closest attention. He thought:
'I'll send a nerve specialist to them this very day.'

"It began when my teeth had to be drawn. There
was nothing to be done about it. They were all hanging loose. I couldn't eat, and in those days I still
thought one had to. Our old dentist drew them for
nothing—and he wanted to make me a set too, but
I couldn't accept such a present—he's going about
himself in burst shoes. When I came home that afternoon and mamma saw me, she went and sat down
in her armchair and began to sob. I had to console
her too. I thought, she's sobbing for too long. But she
couldn't stop. She went on sobbing for days. It was
really quite mad, for we'd gone through so much
misery already and it hadn't made her sob. But it was
the last straw, and later I used to find her in front of
that nice pastel portrait of me by Kokoschka—the
one where I'm laughing with all my teeth, and then
she'd look at me, and begin afresh. It didn't bother
me particularly: it happened to be holiday time, so
nobody came to see us, and I couldn't see myself
either—it was a long time since I'd looked at myself
in the mirror. I did say to myself sometimes that
when mamma was normal again, we'd have to consider what could be sold so that I could get a set
made.

"But she didn't get normal. Then I said to myself: 'She must have something to divert her mind.' I wanted her to go walking with me and sit somewhere in a park—it was the middle of summer; but I couldn't get her to do that—it was as though she was ashamed when anyone looked at us. But I still didn't understand why. Then once she said: 'But you can't go among people like that,' and I realized she was ashamed to show herself in public with me."

"No, no," cried Otto, "that's impossible! Aunt Paula isn't like that."

"Oh, yes," said Lili, and she nodded her decided, maniacal little nod. "Oh, yes, mamma is like that. In the old days mamma always insisted on having beautiful people and things about her, and she liked to show her beautiful things to others—don't talk—not to show off of course, but because she enjoyed them so much herself and wanted to make others happy too. Of course she didn't want to go into the street with me after I'd grown so hideous. Oh, yes, I'd grown ugly long before that—be quiet now. After all, I'd seen myself grow old in the looking-glass. I'd been an old spinster for years, but she hadn't noticed it. I was her child. But the day I came home without any teeth, then she saw it—everything at once—and it was all over with her. Of course it was all over with me too —when I understood there was no longer any reason to live."

"You've been very foolish, unbelievably foolish,"

said Otto. "There was a reason for you two to live. You don't realize it yourselves, but you're the last, you belong to the last aristocracy of the world. Through you, I can see what I must be. It's for that that women like Aunt Paula and you are placed in the world—simply so that you should live in such a way that others can see you. Not to be looked at with ordinary eyes, dear, foolish cousin—the pretty, well-cared-for film stars serve that purpose—but so that people can see what bearing means—see how you carry yourselves under all circumstances. And now you two have gone to pieces. . . ."

"There was nothing to keep me up," sobbed Lili softly. She sank into the little armchair, a poor heap of faded womanhood. Round about her, on the floor and on the chairs, lay the pitiful remains of an antiquated wardrobe, and Otto understood why: he knew women. He saw from the disorder of her room how feverishly she had tried to make herself a little attractive for his visit. Only now did he realize the hopeless humiliation she must feel in her faded dressing-gown, articulating impotently with her mumbling mouth. Full of warm pity, he put his arm about her shoulders again.

"Oh, I'm talking nonsense. The main thing is that you should take some pleasure in life again. First of all, you must pick up enough strength. This evening in any case I'll eat here. Then I shall see whether I can't get you two going again."

Lili had pressed her head into the upholstered chairback. She shook his arm from her shoulders.

"No, I won't eat any more. It's finished—all over. I've had enough. We don't need to eat any more either. Happily we no longer have to get up to cook meals. We sleep most of the day, and when you sleep you're away from everything. It's wrong to do away with yourself—I want to be buried in our own grave, and I certainly don't want to get into the papers. Just imagine: the Countesses Wernizek-Bolnanyi at the top of the list of gas suicides. That mustn't be. But this just happens of itself. Mother had stopped eating already; she did nothing but sob. So why should I go on cooking? When I grew accustomed to the idea that everything was over, my hunger grew less too. Then I could go on sleeping. Oh, yes, we still drink a glass or two of milk. That's left at the door. It's just enough to let one go on sleeping. But now you've come. When I heard you were coming, everything was suddenly different again. Why need you have come? Now everything's going to begin at the beginning again. You've awakened me, and I've got to think again—"

Otto had to bend down to understand her. She kept her forehead pressed against the upholstered back of the little chair. He laid his hand upon her shoulder and stroked her consolingly, but with an angry gesture she shook him off.

"I won't think any more," she cried with a catch in

her voice. "Leave me. Then I can go to bed. Stay away. Don't come back again. You're making everything much worse."

She had jumped up. Her hands drew the dressing-gown higher around her neck where he had touched her with the tips of his fingers. Her pupils drifted strangely away in the white of the eyes. Otto noticed it; he knew the symptom through his brother who was in the sanatorium. 'No, no,' something within him cried. 'Not that. That mustn't be,' and recovering his capacity for action he seized Lili by the hand.

"Listen!" He looked straight into her eyes until they saw him again. "This is not to be, I won't have it. You're to dress at once, and you'll come out with me into the streets, teeth or no teeth, and you'll buy what you need to cook for me this evening. At once! I shall wait for you in the passage, and later I'll come back with a doctor for your mother. I shall take that onyx monster with his golden foot away to sell. You can get twenty sets of teeth for that, and food for at least a year. Francis Joseph, believe me, is no longer in a position to take offense. Are you two so completely God-forsaken that you're allowing yourselves to die slowly, while moldering away in the front room you've got things worth thousands?"

His animal spirits thundered through the room. His words stormed past the ears of the little faded countess. Slowly she raised her eyebrows—for a moment her ageing, shadowed features bore the look of an inquiring child's face. The convulsive, decided little smile tried to come back, but seemed to dissolve instead. Soft and astonished, her lips parted. For the first time, she was fully aware that the man who stood there was Otto von Wernizek, her younger cousin, her shy adorer in the days of her prime, the gallant brotherly comrade in later years, but above all the friend she had missed so long, the friend to whom she could say everything because he understood the promptings and the urges that beat in the blood of the Wernizeks. Only now did she realize that he had come, that he wanted to help her because they were related.

At that moment, a pain shot through her body that was worn out with sobbing, with thinking, that had been exhausted for months. Whence came this grief? From what prison had it escaped? Now it had broken out unexpectedly. It overwhelmed her, making her heart beat as though it would burst. The heart she had carried about empty so long was suddenly filled with pain. Somber grief flowed over her, welled up in an irrepressible flood of tears. Then she put her hands before her face and sobbed out her despair.

Filled with a deep, warm pity, Otto looked down upon her. But he was satisfied. He even tried not to console her—it was better so. Poor wretch, sob your heart out. Sob yourself back into the world. His eyes stood large with compassion, but he did not touch her. He knew women. She had no need to suffer more than was strictly necessary—and he had felt how irritably she had shaken off his hand a while ago.

"That's right. That's better," he said quietly when Lili's shoulders ceased to shake. Her tears were still flowing, but slowly and beneficently as rain on a summer's evening. "You needn't go out into the street with me. Just sit here quietly. I'll come back presently. Now I'm going to find a psychiatrist for your mother, and order our evening meal. The Goldene Pfau will send it round. Tidy yourself a little, Lili. You can't receive the doctor like that."

Outside her door he took a deep breath. God! Life was too difficult for people.

Ora pro nobis. He put his hand over his eyes. He felt like dropping dead with exhaustion. Was this the home-coming to which he had looked forward for so long? He knew now that all the time he had only half dared believe in a home-coming. He felt that he had fondly deluded himself with a deliberately manufactured fictitious fulfillment of his wish for a home that awaited him—a real home of his own such as the poorest peasant finds when he puts away his spade and the day's work is over. Apparently it was no longer given to a Wernizek-Bolnanyi to found a home in this world. . . .

But then he shook himself. No self-pity, please! Of course he was dead tired: traveling all night and not one emotionless moment since—who could have stood that?

'The first thing to do is to go and smoke a cigarette in the Burggarten,' he thought. 'The jasmine is certainly still in flower.'

When he passed through the sitting-room, his aunt was no longer there, but behind the door of the bedroom he heard the bed crack. The sound made him unreasonably furious. He could have struck the furniture with his fists. But he only seized the pompous onyx bowl, and wrapped it angrily in the tissue paper that was still lying there from his flowers. Mr. Haymaker's secretary was no rich American uncle. He had just enough travel money with him—no more. 'Sell it for its gold value,' he said to himself, 'and then fetch the best man in Vienna for Aunt Paula—if he's willing to come. Hell! I'll drag him with me.'

He still had plenty of work before him on this first day of his holiday, but before he left he picked up the white lilies carefully one by one from the table where he had laid them down. He gathered up the princely sprays. Then he went to Lili's door, knocked, and stretched his hand with the flowers round the door. "With my deepest respects, dear cousin—and put them in water at once; they're languishing for it."

The little iron chairs that were for hire in the Burggarten were all occupied by a select public. A number of strangers were walking and sitting in the former imperial garden too: the wives of the American Rotarians were there, parading the expensive bought

143

elegance of Viennese *haute couture*. Otto carefully avoided the fashionable promenade, and found against the ivy-clad terrace of the Hofburg a stone bench where he could smoke his cigarette in peace.

Yes, the jasmine was in bloom. Birds were flying in and out of the thick groove, sometimes brushing past his ears, their wings fluttering as they chirped happily in the sunny air everywhere above and about him and rising up towards him in waves out of the warm grass. A few poverty-stricken children were running in a circle on the lawn, clasping each other's little hands. Their rags revealed the lines of their thin but unspoilt childish bodies, and they laughed in small high-pitched voices. A stout, peaceful mother stealthily gave her infant the breast behind a hedge, while her dirty fox terrier guarded the shopping-bag conscientiously between its front paws.

A delicate gray cloud spiraled upwards from the cigarette. Otto followed it with his eyes as it grew fainter and fainter, dissolving in the blue air. Slowly his convulsively controlled nerves relaxed. Something inside him relaxed too—he did not know what. He only felt that, warmed through and through by the sun, he was drifting away on the fragrant atmosphere, drifting away in a rising spiral out of himself and his cares. He was still very tired, more exhausted even than when he left his aunt's, but with a tiredness that could be borne very contentedly while the sun shone on the blossoming jasmine and a soft wind wafted to him waves of scented happiness from a bed of bright red roses.

The stout mother wrapped up her infant again. The fox terrier, relieved of its responsibility for the shopping-bag, came towards the man who sat there so contentedly. It sniffed at the toes of Otto's shoes, and raised towards him a pair of dark, understanding eyes.

"Yes, eh?" Otto rubbed the terrier thoughtfully behind its ears. "It's not so bad here. We've found a good place, old boy." The little dog allowed itself to be fondled with quiet enjoyment. It had not been mistaken: this man knew what was due to an animal. "Now then, you must be getting along with your mistress," said Otto, and exchanged a look of friendly understanding with the kindly owner as she set her perambulator in motion.

Yes, this was his own Vienna. Otto smiled quietly to himself. Then, abruptly, he got to his feet again. He extinguished his cigarette-end under the sole of his shoe, and put the package containing the onyx bowl under his arm. It was heavy, and also it embarrassed him a little to go walking along the Ring with it. So he decided to get rid of it as quickly as possible.

'I'll go to Steiner,' he thought. 'He doesn't give much, it's true, but at least he knows me. I might perhaps get into difficulties elsewhere.'

Steiner the jeweler still tried to maintain his position in his large shop in the Kärntnerstrasse. Though thinner, and gray, he retained the courtly, subservient, obliging demeanor with which in the old days he had got round the court circles of the Hapsburgs, and with which since 1918 he had imposed upon the new rich whom the Viennese tourist industry was sedulously bringing from all countries. He recognized Otto immediately—he always seemed to know by intuition exactly how to place all the bearers of great names with their appropriate rank and title. Otto pushed the onyx bowl towards him.

Herr Steiner picked it up appraisingly in both hands. "A magnificent piece of work in its time," said he.

"Will you buy it from me for its gold value?" asked Otto point-blank.

The jeweler was in no hurry. He examined closely the carving round the bowl, then the chasing on the golden foot, and shook his head dubiously.

"It's very difficult these days to find an amateur for this kind of thing. I don't mind weighing the gold, though. But then I shall have to detach the bowl: d'you mind?"

"Not at all," declared Otto. The jeweler jerked the pieces apart and Otto looked on calmly: he had an aversion for the pompous imitation baroque of the last imperial period. Besides, he had been through the last year of the war too young, straight from the Cadet school in fact: that lugubrious close of the period.

146

"About four thousand schillings worth of gold," said the jeweler, carefully replacing the cover over the scales. "Forgive me, Count—but I cannot offer more than 90 per cent of the gold value. Who knows how long it will be before I can find a buyer? If some amateur should come along, of course I shall get rather more—but you will agree that I'm entitled to something for the risk of losing my interest."

Otto had no need to consider the matter. Of course he would accept the offer. This very day he was determined to send the best psychiatrist in Vienna to Aunt Paula—and who did anything here in these days without immediate payment? "If you can pay me cash, the bowl is yours," he said.

The jeweler bowed politely, went to his strong-box, and counted out the banknotes in a neat little roll. "Are there any historical particulars attached to the piece?" he asked with an air of innocence. He had an idea he remembered something, but wanted to be sure.

"There are," said Otto, "but they're not included in the price. If you want to hear them, you must pay for them." He stood before the jeweler biting his lips grimly. When he looked up, his own face was looking at him from a gleaming polished silver tray, and at once he knew: that was America. Thank God, then, America had been useful for something.

"No, Heaven forbid!" said Herr Steiner. "I can't pay a schilling more; but it would be very kind of you if you would tell me. Perhaps today or tomorrow some American or other may come into my shop wanting to buy a typical piece, and would set store by the particulars."

"Raise your price by ten per cent, and I'll give you a certificate of origin."

"Then I may mention your name?"

"Yes," said Otto, "if the name's worth enough, it can be mentioned."

I'M going upstairs," said Mother Hodl. "You're not!" and Johannes pushed her back onto her decorated chair. "They can do very well without you. If Poldi's managed to bring five children into the world safely, the sixth will arrive all right too."

"But I was there each time before," protested the old woman.

"Then this time she can try without your directions," decided Hodl. "Woman, do you think things only go right when you're about?"

"But, mother," said the eldest son soothingly, "you can't just walk away from here. They can manage very well upstairs without a grandmother, but we can't celebrate a golden wedding here without the bride."

That was an argument indeed, and Resi allowed herself to sit down again on her chair. She was rather worried, but the uniqueness of the situation was beginning to penetrate to her. Her youngest daughter Poldi, wife of Bergmann the head clerk and mother of five dear little girls under ten, had just gone back to her flat on the second floor in order to gladden her parents upon their feast day with yet another present. It seemed that she was to be confined of her sixth child upon this very day. She had got up from the mid-

149

day meal with a pale but smiling face, and had sent Herr Bergmann at once to fetch the midwife.

Father Hodl chuckled at this synchronization of family events, but Mother Resi was anxious. What does a man know of such things? Five times it may go right, but the sixth something may go wrong. She was rather angry with her bridegroom as he sat looking about him genially and listened to the little jokes that were being fired off everywhere in the crowded room. In spite of this sudden event, he remained in a perfectly sunny frame of mind. Yes, and why not? Father Hodl took the world as it was, with its good days and its bad, with its births and its deaths, with all that it gave.

Today had brought this confinement, but it had also brought wine and cigars and pastry, and the kindly warm gaiety of a large family each member of which knew everything about the others. The good-natured, indecent little jokes were very acceptable between brothers and sisters who had slept three in one bed and in each other's warmth until they had left the house as grown-ups, and the sons- and the daughters-in-law shared automatically in this family intimacy. But the third generation had to keep a little in the background; and they did it too, tactfully. Besides, it was terribly oppressive in the crowded, smoke-filled room, and the youngest ones were delighted to be banished to the spacious entrance hall with its cool tiles, where they were now singing to their mandolins, guitars, and ukuleles all the camping songs that the red and Catholic youth organizations had brought into fashion. Their elders did not listen to them—did they call that singing? They stuck to the *Marriage of Figaro* and the *Merry Widow*.

The young Marias and Resis removed the used coffee cups and refilled the cake dishes. They emptied the overflowing ashtrays and carefully brushed away the crumbs from the white tablecloths. Hodl himself prepared to tap the little barrel of good white local wine that he had obtained at a low price from a friend who owned a vineyard in Grinzing. Three o'clock—and the parish priest of Mariahilf had promised to come before vespers. In the entrance hall Franzl the foreman, who had served Johannes Hodl for thirty years and was still rotund and rosy-cheeked though bald, was putting straight the garlands that had sagged; and the family orchestra tacitly refrained from playing the red youth songs: why put anyone out when it was not necessary?

They were just full-throatedly singing Andreas Hofer's song when Maria Ritter came sailing down the stairs in full pomp, with Josephine a thin dark shadow behind her.

"Good afternoon," said Maria, waving. She meant to escape as quickly as possible from the inharmonious cacophony: but then she noticed the agreeable, fresh young faces of the musicians. "God in heaven!" said Maria as she looked closely at their

151

outlandish instruments. "What's all this?—what a thing!" She took a strange, banjo-like instrument in her hand, and thrummed upon it, bending her head sideways, listening with an expert ear. Grimacing, she returned it to its owner, but all the same she lingered a moment in the midst of the racket that broke out afresh. It was a fine sight, all those young healthy faces, the red cheeks and curling locks of Hodl's descendants. But when a pert, assured saxophone began to sound, she fled to the reception room, and Josephine followed two steps behind her.

The old Hodls stood up, for Maria was a guest of honor. She had dressed accordingly: she was wearing her handsome white fox across her shoulders, and her afternoon dress of black crepe flowed out in distinguished style. Yes, Maria Ritter could still wear her clothes. It was a great moment for Father Hodl: who, thirty years ago, would have dared predict that the great Maria would one day be a guest in his house? Gratefully he bowed over her hand, which he held in his at least ten times longer than Mother Resi thought necessary. Maria was given a chair beside him—and he was lost to all other conversation. He could not resist telling Maria where and when, and in what parts, he had admired her. As he grew more talkative, he recalled opera after opera. He enjoyed himself, he smiled, he gave imitations; and the good Maria listened with rapt attention to her simple admirer: she still knew how to take human beings as

152

they were. Perhaps that was why, in her proximity, he seemed to transcend himself.

Certainly Johannes Hodl might have been a charming and humorous raconteur if life had not made him a stolid master-painter and house-owner. He threw himself into his subject with such gusto that he did not notice how quiet it had become around him, until Resi, with an emphatic wrench at his sleeve, recalled him to his surroundings: and there he suddenly stood face to face with the parish priest.

The parish priest, broad, still not altogether gray, and very virile in spite of the skirt of his soutane, was all joviality and friendliness. He had had to free himself from many irksome little duties in honor of this afternoon. Yes, nodded Resi, it's anything but a quiet parish, Mariahilf. But he would not have liked to miss this festivity. He looked around the circle of respectful or merely inquisitive faces, nodded emphatically to one here and there, and lit with pleasure the extra-special cigar that Hodl had kept apart in his own cigar case, apparently for this purpose. He was well aware that he was one of the turns on the festive program, and was not averse to this—he was used to it, it was part of his parochial duties. This particular duty was, as a matter of fact, nothing but a pleasure, for the parish priest was Vienna-born too, and felt pleasantly at home in this ground-floor dwelling, with the low ceiling still supported by heavy, old-fashioned oak beams. The parish of Mariahilf boasted many similar dwellings, and the parish priest was very proud of them. When he had friends lodging with him, he took them to all the old pot-houses of the Wienzeile so that he could boast of their woodwork and sculpture, and it never bothered him if in the course of these expeditions he came upon places or among people that could not be called exactly virtuous: were not all souls precious to God?

But among the souls of the Hodl family, he felt completely at home. He smoked his cigar compla-cently, and young Resi (whom he had baptized) re-ceived a grateful little wink when she poured an extra portion of cream into his coffee. Yes, yes, the parish priest liked a cup of coffee well enough, but he would not refuse a good glass of wine a little later on; and there was a certain tenderness in the way that the entire Hodl family watched their priest enjoying the good things offered him. A deputation came from the mandolin orchestra to play something in the room, and the boys flushed to the backs of their ears when the parish priest complimented them. On their return to the entrance hall, the rest of the musicians beamed with delight at the success of their comrades.

The parish priest was about to raise his glass to the happiness of the bridal pair, and to speak a few solemn though heartfelt words, when the foreman ap-peared in the doorway and with urgent gestures beck-oned Hodl's eldest son from among a group of argu-mentative smokers. Resi noticed and darted forward,

154

her anxious mother's heart beating fast. Surely nothing was going wrong with the confinement? Hodl too stood up, for the music in the entrance hall broke off, one instrument after the other. Everyone craned his neck—only the parish priest sat on calmly behind his glass: he was sixty-five and had long ceased to feel curiosity.

Across the threshold stepped a very tall, very official-looking gentleman clad entirely in black. 'What dignity,' thought Resi, but then she noticed that the black was no longer so very black, and, having recovered from her first fright, she waited quietly on events.

The gentleman raised his top-hat slowly from his head. His eyes searched the room with the certainty of the expert until they found the bridal couple. Then he took a large package wrapped in green serge from the hands of the man following him—he appeared to be a subordinate person and wore merely a derby hat —posted himself before Hodl and his Resi, and smiled benevolently down on them.

"Somebody from the Registrar's Office," whispered Hodl's eldest into his father's ear. "They came in a municipal car."

"Mr. Hodl and Madam," began the gentleman, "respected bridal pair, I have the pleasure of representing the municipality of Vienna, of which you form a part, in wishing you happiness on your golden wedding feast." At the same time, he threw back the cover, and everyone saw the well-printed, massively framed document he presented to the bridal couple: it bore an impressive photo of the town hall, under which were the words: "Johannes Hodl and Maria Theresa Moller, united fifty years in Wedlock."

"This is extraordinary," declared Hodl. "I hadn't expected this." He shook both envoys of the municipality heartily by the hand. He was not particularly pleased with the municipal authorities, but this was really very nice. Young Maria was bringing forward chairs, but the tall gentleman waved her suavely away.

"No, dear young lady, we shall not sit down. Alas, we have no time. We have to pay seven similar visits this afternoon." Maria was taken aback, and Father Hodl, wounded, slipped back into his breast-pocket the case of special cigars.

"But you'll have a glass of wine," urged Johannes junior.

"You must forgive us, we really can't begin to do that," said the polite official, smiling. The circle of faces about him grew noticeably cooler. He coughed, stuck his hand into an inner pocket, and produced a large white envelope bearing the seal of the city.

"I have also been instructed to hand over this envelope to you. In it you will find the present from the community that is your due. It is a very pleasant task to me to hand this to you, confident as I am that you will know how to make suitable use of it."

156

The envelope was handed to Hodl, and he accepted it with no more than a nod. Then he laid it upon the table. He said nothing, nor did he make any further offer—this was an official event of whose etiquette he was ignorant. He therefore continued to wait for what his visitors would do next.

But they seemed to have accomplished their task. The tall official shook hands once more with Hodl and Resi, bowed suavely on all sides, and departed, preceded by the eldest son. Bending, he edged his top-hat safely under Hodl's door. The subordinate official in the derby hat, having folded the green serge in its creases, disappeared behind him without salutation: he was evidently no more than a walker-on.

When the municipal car, tooting, had started off, Hodl junior and the foreman looked at one another questioningly, shrugged their shoulders, and went inside again. There Father Hodl had torn open the envelope: it contained a note of a hundred schillings.

"Well, would you believe it?" he said to the parish priest. "They've returned my own miserable taxes to me!"

But the parish priest was a righteous man. "Oh, I've seen that sort of thing before at a golden wedding: a poor couple can make good use of the money. The Emperor used to send a little present with his good wishes to needy couples on their golden wedding day, and it's rather nice the municipality should keep up a good custom. But whether you, Mr. Hodl, would have come within the terms in those days, is another question."

"Yes," said Hodl, "it's easier for the authorities just to send round to everybody. Will you do me a favor? Take this money for your poor. Then I shall know for certain that it'll go where it was meant to."

"But with the greatest pleasure in the world!" The parish priest's whole face beamed. His way of accepting a gift was extremely gratifying. His church was never short of flowers, his poor never suffered more hunger than was inevitable in these days—and his parishioners experienced the bliss of giving. "Now I shall be able to make several happy this afternoon," said the parish priest, as with slow deliberation he opened his heavy pigskin briefcase. Every member of the Hodl family could see that the money was being put away for the poor by their parish priest.

"Now a little more music," ordered Hodl, "and more wine too, Johannes. Jesus, that fellow's left a poor sort of taste in my mouth!"

Johannes junior poured, first for Maria Ritter, then for the parish priest, then for his father; and finally he filled the empty glass that thirsty Josephine held out to him without making any excuses.

"And now, dear friend, are we not to have the pleasure of hearing you once more?" The parish priest, who had been sitting at some distance from Maria, did not want to leave without saying an amiable word to his faithful confessant. Besides, he

158

had rather pleasant memories of a charity concert at which she had appeared years ago.

"If you come this evening, you'll hear Frau Ritter," declared Hodl proudly. "She's promised to sing an aria or two to us. But, now I come to think of it, what shall we do about the accompaniment?"

Strangely enough, Maria had not thought of that either. She had grown accustomed to accompanying herself; but when she considered the matter, she would certainly have liked to sing standing this evening—perhaps even act a little too.

"We've got a piano of sorts," said Johannes, "but nobody plays on it now."

"Well, in that case I'll bring someone with me," promised Maria, thinking of Paul Wolùk: she would draw the boy from his loneliness, whether he would or no. A bath in this innocent, friendly happiness would do him good. "I'm sure I know someone, and here in your own house too, away at the back, Herr Hodl."

"That sour face? He'll certainly not come. He scarcely looks at a man," remarked Hodl.

"He'll come if I ask him," Maria assured him, and thereby bound herself to produce Paul Wolùk that evening.

"But he's a violinist, isn't he?" asked Hodl, still dubiously.

"The boy plays the piano too when necessary. I know him." Yes, Maria liked to triumph where others

159

failed; and the parish priest smiled secretively. He had often had to stand by his forceful parishioner and pick up the stitches she so rashly dropped, but— that was the sort of little job for which he existed in the world.

By this time the room was cram-full; they were standing on one another's toes. From the Luftbad-gasse, which had finished its mid-day meal and even done the washing-up, came a constant stream of mothers with their children to offer congratulations. The children all wanted to enjoy a *Hirschhörnchen,* and their mothers wanted to enjoy a little glass of something too. Cigar smoke hung blue above their heads, and the heat—convivial though not fragrant —increased every minute. Maria had hung her fox fur behind her. She had no thought of going yet; but the parish priest started up when the house clock shrilly struck four, adjusted his soutane, and prepared to take leave.

Even thicker grew the hedge of people pressing in to offer their congratulations. It was scarcely possible to get through them, and the young girls gave up trying to remember whose cup and whose glass was whose. They posted themselves by the door and poured out for everyone who offered a drinking vessel. Johannes junior, who had inherited his father's stature as well as his repose and assurance, stood by to supervise. When Meyer Jonathan, returning from his day's work, crossed the entrance hall to offer the bridal pair his good wishes before climbing the three flights to his flat, he saw no possibility of thrusting his way through the compact mass of people inside the room. There he stood, silver white and small, helpless but smiling, behind a wall of backs; and good-natured Franzl had to precede him and make a passage for him by force before he was able to offer his hand to Hodl.

But just at the same moment the parish priest had put out his hand to take leave, and so the two of them stood before Hodl, who went through a difficult moment; but Meyer Jonathan withdrew his hand—an ecclesiastic obviously took precedence. Still, Hodl's friendly heart was not satisfied. With his left hand, he seized Meyer's bony little hand and gave it a warm sturdy grip. "Thank you for your good wishes. Thank you for coming." Smiling, the three old men stood a moment with hands joined.

Then Johannes pushed in front of the parish priest towards the door, for he wanted to escort this guest to the frontiers of his domain. Meyer Jonathan followed behind the parish priest's broad back, and so reached unharmed and without effort the less crowded entrance hall. But there they remained standing, the three of them. From the main gate, loud voices resounded. The foreman, articulating with emphasis, was answering a stream of shrill though incomprehensible nasal sounds; while outside in the street a klaxon kept giving penetrating signals.

"What can that be?" asked Hodl, and listened perplexed to the strange word-duel his usually peace-loving foreman was conducting with a cocksure gentleman in yellow-brown tweeds who flourished two gesticulating hands in Franzl's face. "I can't make head or tail of it. What's the man saying?" asked Hodl, turning to the parish priest.

"It seems to be English," declared the parish priest.

"What's the fellow want?" bawled Hodl to the foreman.

"Do I know?" Franzl shouted back over all the heads. "I don't understand a word."

"Unless I'm mistaken, it isn't English after all," reported the listening parish priest: once upon a time he had had lessons from a man who had studied at Oxford. Meanwhile, the man at the main gate stood stamping his feet in growing excitement, waving nervously in protest towards the street, where a car continued to emit penetrating signals of impatience.

"It's surely a man from the films," remarked the platinum-blond cousin, and sure enough a handsome film camera was hanging from the shoulders of the stranger.

"Does anyone here speak good English?" The parish priest directed the question into the inner room, and immediately Maria Ritter got up full of interest. Yes, she spoke English. She had never learned it, but she had toured England and America, and had sometimes conducted very intimate conversations with British gentlemen who, as is well known, disdain to understand any language but English. Maria therefore pressed forward, and yes, she understood a little; but then she laughed in the parish priest's direction.

"That's not English, it's Yankee-doodle." She pushed nearer; but just as she was about to enter the now feverishly heated atmosphere between Franzl and the American, a loud sound of rejoicing arose on the back stairs where Herr Bergmann, the expectant father, stood flourishing both his arms. His normally expressionless head-clerk's face shone with excitement and perspiration.

"It's a boy, a boy!" he shouted down the stairs, and the whole company waved back at him with raised arms. Mother Hodl climbed the stairs. She threw her arms round his neck and gave him a resounding kiss on his moist red face, and new rejoicing reverberated through the entrance hall. Old Hodl also turned away from the intruder. He raised a *Hoch*. The whole wedding party rejoiced with him, and the nearest neighbors came rushing up. The parish priest enlightened them. "The christening will be today too," he beamed, and all the bystanders smiled agreement.

But poor Mr. Hunter, who had come to invite Otto von Wernizek—if need be to lay him under requisition—for an expedition to the river baths, felt more and more helplessly at sea among this incomprehensible chaos. His nether lip sagged limply. He could almost have cried. Was there nobody he could reach with words? For even the lively stout lady who had been on the point of coming to his aid had turned away again and was standing waving her arms and pressing forward. Then a tray of glasses filled with wine was brought, and everyone made ready to drink a health. Never before had Mr. Hunter felt himself so inefficient, so handicapped.

With a despairing movement of the arm, he was about to seek refuge in flight, when he was suddenly brought to a standstill by a wrench at his coat-collar, and was driven back into the fire again.

"Film them, you fool, film them!" It was Mr. Haymaker who, stamping with impatience, stood beside him. Yes, Mr. Haymaker was an artist. He saw things that eluded the cable manufacturer. From his car, he had noticed the decorated façade, and when he reached the entrance hall he felt himself brimming over with excited amusement. The fragrant garlands of green fir and the enthusiastic faces, the raised glasses and the merry jubilation intimated to Mr. Haymaker that he was witnessing good earthly exuberance such as would never come to America again.

"But look about, you misery!" shouted Mr. Haymaker, pointing towards the group of people from which the parish priest, impressively full of good humor, was detaching himself. "Fire away! First him." And Mr. Hunter began to turn about while Mr.

Haymaker directed operations, pointing this way and that—to small wrinkled Meyer Jonathan: a museum piece, that little Jew—to the beamed ceiling with the colored scutcheons and the Chinese lanterns—to the apprentice who was holding his coffee cup on the sly under the tap of the beer barrel—to the swaying, noisy orchestra, to Hodl's square head which stood out like a beacon above the jostling crowd, to the thin Josephine who, obviously full of good wine, was dancing a *pas-seul*, her skirts lifted with both hands, her little finger pointing upwards.

Hunter twisted and turned. He had difficulty in keeping pace with Haymaker's instructions. Then the roll of film came to an end, and he could let his tired arm fall. He tried once more to attract the attention of those about him, but nobody paid any further heed to him. Apparently they had given up trying to unravel the problem of his presence: there was too much else that demanded their interest.

"But are these people stark, staring mad?" asked Mr. Hunter, when Franzl, whom he had tried to seize as he hurried past, shook off his grasp impatiently. "They might at least say something. You try, Haymaker."

Haymaker considered the situation with his sharp eyes. Then he whistled softly between his teeth and gave Hunter a roguish sidelong glance. "I've a marvelous introduction for you, Hunter. Do you see that stout old lady over there? Twenty years ago she was the greatest coloratura singer in the world—Maria Ritter. In the days when I was still third conductor in Chicago I had to show her round the town. Alas! she hasn't grown prettier, sonny—but she certainly speaks English. I'll hook on to her for you."

And Mr. Haymaker with his best European manners descended upon Maria Ritter. Bowing deeply, he reminded her of their earlier acquaintance, and with due ceremony introduced the former royal and imperial court singer, Frau Maria Ritter, to Mr. Hunter of Midland. Maria assumed once more for this occasion the bearing of a diva; as though clad in costly even if theatrical ermine, she stood with an almost princely dignity before the cable manufacturer, the mere man of commerce.

"Two continents have offered their ovations to Madame," declaimed Haymaker, who knew what was due to a performing artist.

Thus he gave Maria the opportunity to ask: "In what way can I be of service to you, gentlemen?"

"Can you tell us what is the origin of this most delightful spectacle?" asked Haymaker.

But Hunter pushed him on one side and said: "I've come for Mr. Wernizek."

"Well," said Maria, "I saw Count von Wernizek go out a short while ago. He's certainly not at home."

Mr. Hunter's lower lip fell dejectedly; he looked like a deeply disappointed child. But Haymaker was enjoying a silent triumph. He had urgently advised

166

Hunter to leave Otto alone, but the man had refused to be diverted from his purpose—he was determined to be fully informed when he appeared before his friends in Midland.

"Try again after dinner," advised Maria. "He'll probably dine with his family on his first day, and then you'll see something more of our golden wedding too. The merry-making begins in earnest this evening."

"Can it be even worse?" growled Hunter.

"Worse?" asked Maria, wounded, and Haymaker hastened to assure her that he appreciated this cheerful gathering beyond measure and would like nothing better than to spend an hour or so in it.

"But of course," said Maria, nodding. "Come and look on this evening. This is old Vienna as you'll never see it on the stage. And if you'd care to contribute some little attention for the bride, I'll introduce you as my guests. . . . I too am going to oblige the company."

"That's charming," answered Haymaker, smiling, now quite sure he would not take advantage of the invitation. He therefore said: "If I'm not unexpectedly prevented, you'll see us appear about nine o'clock."

"Splendid!" said Maria. In her active brain a scheme was already ripening: she would introduce Paul Wolùk to this Mr. Haymaker, who seemed to have made a success of his career.

"Till this evening then," said Mr. Haymaker, convinced that he would never again see Maria Ritter in this life.

"Till this evening," growled Mr. Hunter, firmly determined to make Otto, the only Viennese with whom he had so far been able to talk, serve his future plans. "Tell Mr. Wernizek we'll look in again tonight."

THE second door key no longer lay under the mat. God be praised! Daniel must have come home. He must be inside, behind the door that Meyer Jonathan tried with trembling hands to open: he found it difficult to slip the key into the lock while his heart propelled happiness so swiftly through his old body. But he succeeded at last, and slipped into the little passage on tiptoe—the boy would surely be asleep after being away from home two nights.

But Daniel was not asleep. True, he was lying on the divan onto which he had dropped when he reached home because he had intended to sleep; but one does not fall asleep just when one chooses to. Worn out and exhausted as Daniel had felt on the return trip from Laxenburg, he became feverishly, tensely awake the moment he stretched himself upon the divan. Instantly, a little buzzing motor started turning in the spot where normally his brain functioned; and in the driving-belt revolved the wheel upon which visual memories of the last two days followed one another over and over again. He was utterly incapable of stopping the motor, and thus was forced helplessly to live over again bit by bit all he had gone through: with this difference, that now it

169

was over he knew precisely what he ought to have said and done on each of those occasions. And at the central point, the hub of the driving-wheel, his own central point, was slowly rotating a leaden dislike for himself, for man in general, for the world, for everything that in and about him thought and willed.

Ever and again one memory returned: the smoky little back-room where he and the Weissensteins and several other students had stood erect opposite Hermann Julius as he enunciated the oath that they repeated with two raised fingers: "I swear at all times and in all circumstances to obey my leader Hermann Julius and to carry out his orders until he releases me from this oath. In case of disobedience, I subject myself to every punishment he may decree." Daniel Jonathan the law student was not satisfied with the wording of the oath. He picked it to pieces, put the pieces together again, played a little with it—all from fear of handing over his thinking apparatus to the other Daniel Jonathan, the real living Jonathan who was waiting to ask the one great, cardinal question: 'Why did you in fact take this oath?'

'Why did you take the oath?' The question finally prevailed over his buzzing, whirling thoughts. Now it had to be answered. 'Because the ruffians who threw Walter through the window must be given a lesson.' It was purely a defensive organization that Julius had intended to found. 'And yet subsequently they contrived to get hold of Fritz Weissenstein.' True.

170

And that was one reason the more for taking revenge. 'But that could quite well have been done without the oath to Hermann Julius. Why have you surrendered yourself body and soul to another?'

Each time he reached this point Daniel's capacity for thinking continually stopped working. Well, he had surrendered himself, and that was the end of it. One should not ask too many questions; the Weissensteins and himself and all the others had nothing to ask when they lifted Walter's shattered limbs from the cobbles. They could only do something, do something together, do it as well as possible so that such a horrible thing could not happen again. Julius was there. He was the eldest and had already led a group in Hanover. Surely there was only one possibility of serving a cause—to surrender oneself to it, body and soul.

'Julius isn't a cause. He's a human being.'

Ah, why had Daniel a Meyer Jonathan as grand-father? Why did he spring from a line of indefatigable Torah researchers, subtle seekers after truth above all else? He could find no rest for his ever-questioning spirit. "Thou shalt recognize no gods but me. . . ." He was doomed continually to live over again, to re-consider his deeds—good or bad, thoughtless or in-tentional—and he could find no rest. He tossed from left to right and from right to left on the narrow divan; and when for an instant his bewildered thoughts knotted themselves into a state bordering on

171

unconsciousness, suddenly the realization pierced his heart that over there Rasser and Derresch were lying gasping in the slow martyrdom of suffocation.

This thought it was that over and over again made him start up and drove sleep from his body. Oh, Rasser and Derresch were scoundrels, cads, murderers; but in every nerve of his sleepless body Daniel experienced the terror and the torment that was being endured at that very moment away in Laxenburg. Constantly he reminded himself: 'They deserve it because of Fritz.' But immediately the strangling truth gripped him again: 'They're lying there because you will it, because you let them lie there. Can you bear that?'

'Julius wills it.'

'No, it is you yourself. You took the oath,' and again ineluctably the question rose: 'Why did you swear that oath?'

Daniel turned over again, incapable of answering the question. He clenched his fists; he simply refused to think any more. An oath was an oath, and whoever had once taken it was bound. The only thing that remained to do was to accept the consequences of the oath.

Daniel stretched himself to the full length of the divan. His arm and knee joints cracked. He felt his own measure. Yes, this was a decision. He could live by it without questioning: to accept the consequences of his own deeds.

He opened his eyes, and at last banished all hope of some hours of dreamless sleep: it was useless to lie waiting for something that did not come. He got up from his bed. When he saw by his watch that it was already four o'clock, he was alarmed—he had come home at half-past eleven. He had therefore been lying for four and a half hours in the grip of his revolving thoughts. What happened next?

He stood in the middle of the room without wish, without purpose. His eyes were vacant and yet strained between their burning eyelids. His glance fell upon his writing-table, the small, overcrowded writing-table of the poor student. In the middle of the blotting paper lay the shining French revolver: the thought occurred to him that here was the accepted manner of escaping one's difficulties. Then he turned away with an indifferent shrug of the shoulders. He stood there between four walls, and endured the senselessness of standing waiting without the emergence of a single impulse.

But then a finger tapped three short raps on the door of his room.

The noise roared like the beat of a drum in Daniel's ears, which for hours had paid no heed to any outside sound. Fear ran over his skin. He trembled, and the reaction from the shock made him feel snappish and defensive towards Meyer Jonathan, who came in and smiled at him, but with ill-concealed anxiety in his eyes.

173

"I heard you get up," said Meyer Jonathan. "Haven't you eaten anything yet, boy? There's nothing lying about, no dish or cup."

"I'd already eaten—that's all right. Just go in; I'll come in to you for a moment before I go out. I want to go and wash now."

Daniel did not look at his grandfather: it was too difficult to look into Meyer's eyes and then resume one's own way. His own way? But did that still exist? . . .

Himmel! what a scatter-brained notion! Of course he would go out into the street again shortly, even though it meant going out without purpose. Things were happening there that he had helped to set in motion, and he wanted therefore to be present. That was all, and that was why he gave no further answer when Meyer Jonathan, after taking a long deep breath, asked gently: "Must you go out again, Daniel?"

He slipped past his grandfather towards the little kitchen. He shut the opaque glass door behind him. Meyer Jonathan followed him down the passage. He stood before the closed door and watched a shadow glide backwards and forwards over the dull white glass. His eyes followed his grandson's shadow, and he guessed that Daniel was now holding his head under the tap above the sink, holding it there an uncanny length of time. He had long ceased to hear the water flowing, and the dark shadow on the opaque

174

glass was still bending over motionless. He could no longer see it, and fled into the sitting-room.

"Well, good-by then." Daniel thrust his head round the door. He knew at last what he would do this afternoon—go to Ladislaus, of course, to borrow the books on Soviet law, and perhaps to chat a while with Ladislaus, who knew of the affair. Yes, he must talk to someone so as to avoid thinking, and he could talk to Ladislaus.

"Daniel!" cried Meyer Jonathan, and with the door-knob in his hand the boy hesitated. The subdued cry sounded hoarse with grief.

"Is anything the matter, grandfather?" he asked from the doorway. But then he looked at Meyer Jonathan, and had to close the door behind him and go towards the armchair where the old man had sat down again, bending forward with his hands resting on his knees as if he were in pain.

"Is anything the matter, grandfather?" repeated Daniel.

Oh, there was so much, much too much, so much that it became unutterable. Meyer Jonathan could only stare into Daniel's eyes, mute and set. His mouth moved, but the "Hear, O Israel" that in all extreme moments welled up to his lips remained unuttered. Only his hands moved upwards, as if searching for something. Then he laid them upon Daniel's shoulders as they bent towards him. He drew himself up by those shoulders, and stood before the boy. Then his

175

hands rose higher until they lay on the dark bowed head of his grandson.

"God make thee as Ephraim and as Manasseh." He used the old formula in which Jacob had blessed the sons of Joseph, in which every Jewish father still commends his sons to God's care when he lays his hands upon them. But Meyer Jonathan was not thinking of Ephraim and Manasseh. He was not thinking at all. He felt Daniel's head under his hand, and his whole soul called down God's blessing upon that beloved head. It was surely permissible to add his own words to the formal blessing, and he prayed: "Not for me, Almighty, not for Thy erring servant, but for him, for the child himself, and for Thy people, O Lord. Save him. Lead him along Thy way in righteousness." And then he uttered the solemn priest's blessing which he, born of the family of high priests, was entitled to give. There was a ring in his voice again as he uttered the precious sacramental words: "May the Lord bless thee, and keep thee. May the Lord make His face to shine upon thee, and be gracious unto thee. May the Lord turn His face towards thee and grant thee peace."

Daniel's head bowed deeper under the blessing hands: how often they had lain so, and how gratefully had he always felt the love of the old man descend into his being, even long after he had rejected the faith of his fathers. But now he could have screamed with uneasiness as the stream of tenderness went over him. As he stood there he seemed to be double, a being split in two; one half moaning and imploring a blessing, the other hostile and longing to flee.

The old man felt his hands slip away from Daniel's head; it had withdrawn itself.

"I'll be going now, grandfather. Perhaps I'll be home this evening after all"—and the door closed behind Daniel.

Meyer Jonathan stared for a long time at the rectangle of the door panel.

At a quarter to five Daniel was standing once more on the little square in front of the Matteottihof. It presented the same aspect as in the morning, except that now the last touring-car of the day was discharging its load. Daniel made no enquiries this time; he stepped at once towards the corridor leading to Ladislaus's flat. Nobody noticed him except one of the older unemployed, who, loitering against a lamp-post, commanded a clear view of Ladislaus's door and windows.

"So you've come," said Ladislaus. He had not doubted for a moment that the boy would come. He was accustomed to his suggestions achieving their purpose, and was only surprised that Daniel had not been on his threshold by a quarter to four. "Take a seat—yes, that's quite solid," and Daniel sat opposite Ladislaus on a creaking three-legged stool, completely at a loss for anything to say.

177

He cast about for an opening, but suddenly his mind became as distracted as it was in the evenings in the inner town among the brilliant shop windows and the moving illuminated signs. From every wall of Ladislaus's room posters large and small shrieked for attention. He did not know which to look at first. Lenin's penetrating eye tried to mesmerize him, his pointing finger to press a watchword into his brain. Elsewhere a red fist was extended towards him threateningly. An engine dragging a swishing tail of tank cars raced forward over an endless right of way; and three tractors drew furrows across a red sky. The monster poster that covered the wall above the whole breadth of Ladislaus's writing-table showed a net of fierce colored lines over a whirl of photos. It seemed intended to represent a system, but in the middle of the web of lines a fierce worker's head gaped open-mouthed, shrieking with frantic delight.

Daniel was too empty and tired to meet this delight with anything except indifference. His gaze returned to Ladislaus, who, thin and ill, sat huddled against the back of his office chair. In Ladislaus's eyes, the dark, deep-set eyes of a consumptive, lay a tinge of mockery as he followed Daniel's reactions.

The boy felt doubly irresolute and confused as he sat opposite this older and undoubtedly important person. He even felt it to have been presumptuous on his part to interrupt contact between this worker and his writing-desk, full of documents, manifestoes,

178

and newspapers. And then suddenly, spontaneously as a child, he surrendered to the respect he at that moment became conscious of feeling for Ladislaus.

Of course Ladislaus was willing to answer the many questions he wanted to ask: he had, after all, been entrusted with propaganda at the university. Therefore he knew the answers to almost every question the law student put about Soviet law and economy. He had also an amazing knowledge of literature. He did not converse, but he gave precise, confidence-inspiring information. He referred to his pamphlets and books when necessary. Daniel pleased him: at least the boy was not afraid of admitting when he failed to understand. Besides, Ladislaus felt almost physically the stream of concentrated attention that issued from him. 'How did a boy like this manage to fall in with that cad of a Julius?' he asked himself; but he evolved no hypothesis—he was accustomed to work with facts.

It had been a difficult school in which Peter Ladislaus, alias Jobson, and before that Molotov, had learnt to limit himself to facts. His physique had not permitted him either to subject his fiery, passionate, idealistic being to his over-acute intellect. Now and then with the blood of his lungs he spat out in bitterness all his repressed emotions. He could have given much good advice to this boy, in whom he saw himself over again, but he would not do it; his only task was to use the boy for the Communist cause, the

179

greatest cause he had been able to find in this world to which to surrender himself and others.

"Then you believe Communism to be the ultimate form society will take?" asked Daniel when, the books under his arm, he had already been standing a quarter of an hour about to take his leave.

"Yes," said Ladislaus, and knew that he did not believe in ultimate forms. But what critical intellect nearing thirty can escape relativity? "Yes, I believe in Communism, in the victory of sound reason. That is, the highest reason. I believe we did not receive our brains in order to let them atrophy. I believe our capacity for thinking is our best weapon, and that we must use it to attack this stupid world; to break down barriers, class barriers, national barriers, race barriers—all the foolish obstructions that stand in the way of a planned world organization. An intelligent human being who dares to think things out is a Communist."

"And what about Social Democracy?" asked Daniel, who had some good friends among the Socialist students, reliable, agreeable comrades.

"Social Democracy is a movement that has come to a dead end," said Ladislaus. "But you must understand me: I'm no simple-minded Socialist-hater like the majority of Communists. I'm too familiar with historical necessities. Young man, the Socialists have done all they can do; they've extracted everything from capitalism for the workers that can be obtained

180

without violence. Mind you, without violence. They've tried to fight the class-struggle without violence, while taking into consideration all the conceptions of respectability dear to a western European—apparently because their grandparents learned them from the Church. Yes, Social Democracy is not a fighting movement. It is barely a movement at all these days. It is standing still. It has reached the end. It can go no farther. It's an island of refuge for the older generation. If it should ever be compelled from below to fight, it will have to fight with us, to adopt our methods." Ladislaus stopped to cough and Daniel waited with averted eyes for the end of this painful intermezzo. Then Ladislaus went on imperturbably: "But most of the European Social Democrats will fight no more, my little friend. They cannot bear to see blood. In this country there are some good elements: they try to realize proportions, but they don't see straight. They've got all the old women of the Second International against them, all the wallowers in emotion who prate of brotherhood and common humanity and international peace."

Ladislaus had overcome his cough. He had talked himself into enthusiasm. "You know, I believe in Communism because I believe in clear thinking, and in doing what one thinks. I see red when I hear the gentleman of the radio talk about a 'fierce struggle' and a 'bravely fought victory' when he's communicating an election result to the worthy voter at his tea.

That's people's ruin. I even prefer people who are clear in their minds as to what they want, though it is only their own personal interest. They know something at least: they know what they're after."

'Julius!' flashed through Daniel's mind. 'He's thinking of Julius!' and immediately he asked the question he had been wanting to ask all this time; the question that at this moment was more important than any other. "What then do you think of our circle —of Julius?"

Ladislaus laid down the paper-knife with which he had been carelessly playing. He put it neatly lengthwise on the pen-tray. "Go and sit down again, friend. You should have come to that long ago. Tell me what you think of it—for to be honest I haven't yet taken the trouble to give any thought to your little show."

Daniel continued to stand in the same spot, but he laid down the books again upon the table. "Listen, Ladislaus. I can say it to you—you aren't Julius— but in that circle I feel like a mouse in a trap. I just fell into it, and can't get out of it. Of course I know quite well why we began it: because we saw Walter broken to pieces before our eyes against the stones; and now we're sticking together because of Fritz Weissenstein, and because God knows what may happen yet. But I see no end; there is no end until we have done one another in one by one."

"And he who lives longest inherits everything," said Ladislaus. "No doubt that will be Julius. My friend, I understand your dangers, but to me they're unimportant. You're all engaged in a little game; you're adolescents still wanting to play robbers. Don't imagine your group can be of use to anyone or anything. No, Jonathan—" Ladislaus had got up and Daniel's eyes were fixed wide open upon his face, for it was an unknown Ladislaus, a strong, self-confident soul that shone through the wasted Mongolian human mask. "Jonathan, I'm not afraid of making victims. Hundreds if necessary—if it must be, you understand —because the cause to which they are sacrificed is worth blood. And because I see no other possibility. I sacrificed countless human beings during the petroleum strike in Texas. One by one I sent them into the fire, let them sabotage and spy, knowing that they were dead men if they were caught. In the Caucasus I had to shoot down a whole village, men and women, because they were rebellious and were infecting my district. Such things you don't do for your pleasure, Jonathan, but they've never given me a sleepless night: they were necessary. The lives of men are a costly currency, one must be sparing of them; but to obtain results one must pay the price. Every statesman and every revolutionary knows that. And so, to return to your question, I think this circle of yours, the whole romantic strike-home boiling of you, ridiculous paltry child's play—and I personally take it very ill that Julius has begun such an individualist joke."

183

"Julius is not such a Communist as you," said Daniel. He was sitting on the rickety stool again, and was feeling dizzy. Ladislaus's last words had filled him with a chilly sense of dejection—all the chillier because he felt every word he heard to be irrefutable, even while Ladislaus pronounced his emphatic judgment.

Ladislaus raised a hand. "One moment, little friend. Julius is a Communist too. We're no sectarians, young man: as in the Roman Church, there is, psychologically viewed, room for everyone among us. On a percentage basis, there are probably just as many good and bad boys in Russia as anywhere in the world; but it is a different sort of goodness and badness from that of Pekin or Paris. In Moscow Julius would have been referred this very day to the GPOE for his individualistic adventure; but in Vienna he is quite acceptable, despite his private enterprises."

"But I had no thought of private enterprises when I took my oath," protested Daniel.

"Probably," agreed Ladislaus. "You're not at all the type for that. Of course you wanted to save the world, didn't you? Like Bayard *sans peur et sans reproche,* you wanted to make straight for the monster. But, my dear friend, you're only fighting against windmills. That's what happens when a man puts his brains out of action and hoists himself on his emotions: they're like a racing car without brakes."

"What must I do?" asked Daniel. It was a relief

184

to be able to ask the question aloud, the question that had been beating like an obsession at regular intervals all day long through his consciousness: what must I do, what must I do?

"Nothing," said Ladislaus. "You must do nothing at all until you know what you want."

"But I've taken the oath. I must do what Julius wants."

"True enough. You must therefore decide first of all whether you want to keep this oath."

Ladislaus directed his sharp gaze into Daniel's brown boyish eyes. He knew what he was doing. Julius was a vulgarian, but this Jonathan seemed to be of the sort that could be tempered by fire: he might turn out a strong, noble weapon.

"Ladislaus!"—Daniel brought himself to say it at last, but softly—"Ladislaus, don't you find it frightfully upsetting that Rasser and Derresch are lying there to die like beasts?"

"No," said Ladislaus. "That feeling doesn't affect me at all. I did the only thing I reasonably could to keep you others out of prison, and with that the matter's over, so far as I'm concerned. I really can't sit down and cry for everybody who these days has to pay the piper. And you must be careful, Jonathan: get rid of your sentimentality before it's too late. I predict that we shall be sitting in the middle of a revolution here within the year, and any man who hasn't got his soulful feelings under his thumb, young

185

man, by then will find himself between the buffers—
and certainly on the way to the gallows. Those gentlemen Rasser and Derresch hadn't much trouble with
their feelings when they castrated Fritz Weissenstein."

"You're right," said Daniel; and knew all the
same with renewed certainty that even Ladislaus's
words could not free him from his blind anxiety
because two people whom he knew, whom he had
touched with his hands, were lying in danger of
suffocation.

"Now I must really get on with my work," said
Ladislaus, pointing to his writing-table. "Just think
things over again, Jonathan, and for the time being
do nothing you're not sure ought to be done. When
in doubt, a man should refrain, as you know." His
eyes were already absorbed in a newspaper article,
his shoulders bent forward, his breast hollowed; and
the hand he extended to Daniel as they parted was,
strangely enough, as moist and chilly as it had been
in the morning.

When Daniel (without the books on Soviet law)
crossed the little square of the Matteottihof at six
o'clock, one of the unemployed men on the other side
detached himself from his lamp-post and slouched
away in the same direction. Nobody looked after him
—there are too many unemployed in Vienna. At the
corner of the Siebenbrunnengasse, he adjusted his
cap, took his hands out of his pockets, and tightened

the knot of his neckcloth. His step grew more resilient. He looked much less down on his luck, and was no longer noticeable in the stream of workers who at that hour were wending their way homewards through the streets of Margareten. But he was in fact unemployed no longer: he was following thirty paces behind Daniel, systematically maintaining the same distance. That and nothing else was his work.

For the time being, it was not heavy. Daniel walked straight on, down the whole length of the Sieben-brunnengasse, as if he were bound for a very definite destination. He crossed the Margaretengürtel and continued miles upon his way through Favoriten. His diligent pursuer felt the hot cobbles through the soles of his cheap black canvas sneakers, but he did not give up. He wisely increased the distance between them to fifty paces—the road through the suburb had grown emptier: there were only occasional groups of houses, and the old cottages here and there among the still unbuilt grass plots assumed an increasingly rural aspect. Then like a flash of lightning the loiterer slipped behind a stationary truck, for Daniel came to a standstill, turned round, and started walking back towards the city with the same purposeful step.

Strange. Daniel had just become conscious that he was on his way to Laxenburg on foot; on his way to Laxenburg. When he left Ladislaus's flat, he had had no definite plans. He was free to go where he liked—home to his grandfather or to some friend's room or even to the National Library. As he walked along the Siebenbrunnengasse, he wondered at which station he should take the Stadtbahn. But as he was considering this, he had relapsed into his own thoughts. He forgot that he wanted to get to the Stadtbahn, and walked on until he discovered himself to be on the way to Laxenburg.

It was hot on the sunny road. Daniel swallowed: he was thirsty. 'A gag between your jaws, two woolen blankets and a tent canvas over your head—how long could you hold out like that without food or drink? Rasser and Derresch were sturdy fellows. They would be able to hold out longer than others. They might very well hold out until they were found. Such trained sportsmen's bodies can withstand a good deal. Yes, that's just it. Such trained sportsmen's bodies therefore lie longer waiting for death if they are not found.'

Daniel hastened his steps. He must go back, get among people. What did he mean with all these sentimentalities? Ladislaus was right: one must use one's understanding. Things done cannot be undone.

What had Ladislaus said?

"You must decide first of all whether you want to keep this oath." Of course, it would be possible to write an anonymous note to the custodian of Laxenburg.

Wait. No. That was not what Ladislaus had meant.

188

He only wanted a man to use his understanding, not to surrender reason and everything else to another, to any other human being. The oath had been taken without sufficient thought; but he must not betray what happened under oath. He could only go to Julius and have himself released from the oath for the future —if Julius were willing.

Daniel hastily retraced his steps. The unemployed man in rubber shoes followed stealthily, but very much on the alert. The manner of the young Jew was decidedly interesting to anyone attaching importance to the comings and goings of a Communist agitator's visitors. The loiterer did not pity himself.

'I'll go home to Grandfather,' thought Daniel. The picture of the quiet living-room with the white head bending over parchments, that fervent bowed head in whose proximity he felt so divinely protected from his own unrest, rose like a peaceful vision in Daniel's mind and bathed him for a moment in serenity. Yes, he would get on a bus or a tram somewhere and go to his grandfather. Perhaps he would be able to sleep tonight, and then tomorrow he would speak to Julius.

He was walking once more through a shopping street in Margareten. He walked past the windows and noticed what was displayed in them. He even halted at the window of an instrument maker, and looked absent-mindedly at the shining objects: vaguely he recognized scissors and tweezers similar to those he had seen at Julius's.

In Julius's instrument case . . . the instrument case. . . .

God! Like a sharp flame a thought shot through him, and filled him with burning anxiety. For a moment he stood upright to his full height. Then he turned and raced back along the street. Anxiety drove him forward: suppose Julius also were on his way to Laxenburg at that moment. After all, had he not found himself on the highroad thither a short while ago? Suppose Julius with his instrument case had gone back! Julius was capable of anything. He had only reluctantly given way to Ladislaus. Julius might at that moment be already in Laxenburg; but he might also go this evening when it was dark. He had been unable to do all he had intended doing. He had been thwarted, and Julius would not stand that. No, a man like Julius would not stand that.

Daniel walked back at the double. Clear in his mind and sure of himself, he was on his way to Laxenburg. At the Laxenburger Allee he could take a bus. He did not quite know what he was going to do there, but that he was going was certain.

But at the Margaretengürtel he was brought to a standstill: the traffic had been held up because the Bundesheer with flying banners and much military music was making one of its demonstration marches through the city. For the first ten minutes there was no possibility of getting through. Daniel therefore remained standing among the people, separated from

190

the other side by a moving wall of gray uniforms, above which rows of tanned, stereotyped profiles under steel helmets bearing an oak leaf had lost all differences of human expression. The citizens along the route, accustomed to the sight, did not look at the faces either—that would have been too tiring. They merely pointed out to one another the cannon and machine-guns and the flaunting colonel on his steed.

Daniel's eyes had long since turned away, but his feet wanted to go further. He had some difficulty in standing still among a group of workers who, grumbling, were waiting until the military demonstration had gone by. He looked round: was there no other way?

Then he saw behind him against the houses a neat, recently installed public telephone booth, blinking with aluminum paint and invitingly empty, with a little leather seat between four glass walls. These cells were an unlucky speculation on the part of the Vienna municipality: the authorities ought to have known that in this city men did not throw away their pennies; but what was a working manager to do when the receipts from his service refused to rise? The new telephone booths waited expectantly on many a street corner, and only at one point in the inner city did they attract adequate custom.

This booth, however, immediately arrested Daniel's attention. It was possible to walk round it, look at the fittings, study the working of the new telephone apparatus; in that time, another company of the Bundesheer had gone by.

And then Daniel was suddenly standing in the booth with a telephone directory in his hand, looking up the number of Ministerialrat Rasser.

At the same moment the unemployed man, who had not for a moment lost sight of him in the crowd, shot into the nearest coffee-house, pushed a police badge under the nose of the astonished waiter, and asked: "Where's the telephone? Quick!" The waiter pointed to a corner next to the refreshment bar. The pursuer dialed a number and said quietly but very distinctly: "This is A-23. Listen in to public booth 94." Then he padded away again on feet shod in noiseless shoes. He was just in time to see Daniel pick up the receiver.

There. Now it had happened. He had done it. "It depends first of all upon whether you want to keep your oath." Well, it would appear he had not wanted to keep it. It had happened: he was free from the oath.

A woman's voice had answered. "Frau Rasser," said the voice. "My son? He's in Klosterneuburg." "No," Daniel had said. "Your son is in the park of Schloss Laxenburg in an old summer-house. He's in danger: you must take action at once. Schloss Laxen-

192

burg. Will you repeat it?" Then he had put down the receiver.

He retreated from the Margaretengürtel, where the Bundesheer was still marching past. Now he could go home to his grandfather. It had happened. He was free. He could eat supper simply and normally with his grandfather as usual, as though nothing lay behind or in front of him. The old man would be happy; he was happy himself, very happy, and terribly tired.

He jumped on a tram and seized the porcelain handle of a strap. Below him the rows of faces nodded at every jolt of the shaking tramcar: tired faces of people with a day's work behind them. Yes, everybody was going home. The day was almost over. His day too was almost over. He must just sit a while with his grandfather—and then he would report to Julius.

On the pavement of the Luftbadgasse strolled Herr Friedemann, the ex-spaghetti manufacturer, while his poodle went for a run. He had plenty of time, and so had the poodle—no corner seemed to be to the dog's taste. Daniel approached, and Herr Friedemann limply lifted one finger—no more was due to a Jew boy. Daniel, however, this evening felt an even completer indifference than usual to the fat money-lender, and passed him without acknowledgment. Daniel need no longer be polite: that time had gone. Now only the true, the real things mattered.

"Wasn't that young Cohen who greeted you?" A

respectable-looking workman touched his cap, and Herr Friedemann who, insulted, stood looking after Daniel, turned round and growled: "Cohen? No. That Sheeny happens to be called Jonathan. Look, he lives there. He's just going in." Then, when his gleaming usurer's eyes observed how attentively the other watched Daniel step through the decorated main gate of Luftbadgasse 12, he came closer and asked mysteriously: "Do you want him?"

HALF-PAST six. The central cash desk at Korngross's was far from being at the end of its day's work. True, all the cashiers had by now handed in their cashboxes, and happily they had not made an abnormal number of mistakes. But not until seven o'clock, an hour after the close of the department stores, when the cashboxes containing change were standing ready again in the safe for the coming day, would Roserl Goldös speak of a record. At the moment, she was to the very last fiber of her body, to the smallest cell of her brain, bent upon her object —to beat the previous record time. Round about her rattled and clattered typewriters and adding machines, one by one rolls of schillings and groschen fell with a dull thud from the remarkable machine that had been specially constructed for Korngross's. Into its funnel disappeared bag after bag of unsorted coins, to emerge on the other side counted and packed. For a full month, Roserl had been proud of this labor-saving machine that had been procured at her suggestion. But it had been in use for six months now, she was accustomed to its fulfilling its duty faultlessly, and she no longer gave it a glance. The girls about it worked, busy and tense, without saying a word, and that too was an achievement for the head: when Roserl Goldös put on that determined face, with the furrow between her eyebrows and the narrowly compressed mouth, she was not to be trifled with.

"How are you getting on, Miss Lanz?" With her fountain-pen ready to initial, Roserl stood behind the chair of her assistant, who wrote and wrote with long hasty strokes. "Another five minutes," pleaded the young girl, thinking: 'Fräulein Goldös is really beginning to get a bit soured already.'

The assistant manager looked round the corner. He wanted to know the figure for the day. "Just five minutes!" snapped Roserl. The sum total for the day could have been ready long ago if Erna Lanz had made better headway; the furrow between her eyebrows deepened.

At that moment the telephone rang; one of the girls answered. "It's for you, Miss Goldös." Roserl had already taken the receiver out of her hand.

"No, I haven't the time now. . . . No, no question of it. I'm in the middle of my accounts. . . . What? You can't manage this evening?—yes, a pity. Another time, eh? . . . No, I can't get away from here before seven . . . (yes, Miss Lanz, give me the total, then I can send it through to the manager's room). . . . No, really, I'm busy. I can't listen any longer. . . . Bye-bye."

Roserl pressed down the apparatus, keeping the receiver in her hand. Then she released the switch-

196

hook. "Central cash desk here. Miss, just put me through to the manager's room." The furrow between her eyebrows was as deep as a cut.

Otto put down the receiver and looked vacantly out through the glass wall of the telephone booth. The little square by the Apollo Theatre lay empty and sunny. Only one or two pigeons were pecking invisible fodder between the cobbles. The warmth of the summer afternoon still hung heavy, and kept the playing children together in the cool shade of the little Ester-hazy park that formed a green oasis on the other side. Under its towering trees, it lay like an island of rest close by the busy Scheidekgasse. Otto was very grate-ful for the broad green treetops upon which he fixed his eyes as he slowly returned to the reality of this unsuccessful first day of his holiday.

'Must I give her up?' That was the first thing he asked himself, but at the same time he knew already that that was a stupid question. So long as he was here in Vienna in her proximity, he would want to see her and speak to her, want to take her in his arms. What came after—well, that just came after. This was only the first of six precious days that lay in front of him. Of course he would see her again and speak to her, and certainly he would take her in his arms. . . . The thought was wonderfully stimulating. It drove his blood warm and swiftly through his body. . . . Oh, it was very understandable that she could not listen to him if she was busy at her work; but she could not get rid of him like that. He would go and wait for her at seven o'clock. In any case, he could explain to her better by word of mouth why he was unable to go out with her into the country this evening, as he would have liked so much to do, why he had to remain with Aunt Paula and Lili. Yes, this evening he could not possibly leave the women alone; the specialist was right, they must be carefully nursed back to normal.

The recollection of the visit of the great nerve specialist gave him a feeling of satisfaction. He had been able to do that at least; and furthermore the good man had been far less exacting than he had expected. The result of the examination was, thank goodness, more hopeful than he had anticipated. True, Aunt Paula would never be anything now except an ordinary, rather delicate little old lady. But Lili could certainly be helped. The specialist would instruct his best assistant to attend her. "She must learn to adapt herself again," he had said. "Is there no work or social activity in which she used to be interested?" But Otto could not remember anything. He had heard once that as a very young girl she had had a sudden whim to become a Franciscan nun, but all girls have a way of imagining they have such a vocation when they are brought from the boarding-school to life in the world. He could not remember that later on she had ever done more than pay her one obligatory visit a week to church.

No, she must find her own way back to life; but during the first days he could stand by her a little. "I can be back from Korngross's by half-past seven and this evening I'll keep them company. I'll keep them awake, even if I have to sing scatsongs to them." He pushed his hat to the back of his head. It was warm in the booth: certainly—but what was he still doing there?

As he stepped out, two people who had been waiting stared at him with undisguised fury. He had, after all, occupied the booth for quite ten minutes, long after he had put up the receiver. He smiled apologetically; and his smiling face apparently disarmed them, for the one who was waiting behind (but it was a lady) looked after him with pleasure as he turned into the little street leading to the Mariahilf church.

It was twenty minutes to seven by his watch when he stood on the little church square. Korngross's lay a hundred yards further on. He was too early. "I'll just look into the church," he decided. That had always been one of his hobbies: never to pass by a church if he could find the time to glance into the interior. Besides, Mariahilf was more than an ecclesiastical building. It was very familiar and very dear to him. Often during his workless years he had rested in its peaceful quiet on his aimless walks through Vienna. He hailed with joy, therefore, renewed sight of its shabby baroque. It was, after all, a church for humble folk. "Mariahilf"—those who needed help slipped through its doors and prayed for the relief of their usually very simple human distress.

Just inside the entrance, where an imitation grotto of Lourdes engrossed the more childlike souls, many a one muttered his ejaculatory prayers and hastened away again through a side door; but some knelt on the dirty paving stones, and the tawny beggar woman who sat huddled in a corner received without stirring the gifts that were extended to her by hands that had grown calm in prayer. Small painted and embroidered gifts and little scraps of paper had been thrust between the railings of the grotto. All bore an inscription: "Maria hilf!" or "Maria hat geholfen!" As Otto came in, a schoolboy was busy sticking a pretty colored card through the grating. "Maria hilf!" And Otto smiled: yes, why should not the Mother of Mercy intervene also when an exacting schoolmaster put questions that were too difficult?

He entered the nave of the church. Its enclosing walls received him with the earthly intimacy of their baroque lines, and the painted domed roof brought a blue-and-pink heaven very close. The smell of incense and old oak, of burning candles and half-faded flowers, combined with the inevitable stuffiness of badly washed clothes, met him like a welcome home. No church in America smelt like that. This was really and truly Europe. Satisfied, he took holy water and

200

then sat down in one of the back pews; he wanted to sit there for ten minutes and feel that he was back. He did not fold his hands—one does not live in an analytical period without paying for it—but he enjoyed to the full his surroundings and the atmosphere. Two peasant women from the Naschmarkt had parked their baskets in the central aisle and were saying a few Hail Marys. 'Is the cow going to calve? or are they praying for an unbelieving son?' Otto asked himself. But it did not really matter. They were praying with such complete faith and surrender that it almost brought tears to his eyes.

From behind an altar, the eternal vagabond came shuffling forward, his hands resting upon that gnarled stick on which his like have leaned since Cain first went wandering. His eyes were bloodshot, his thin beard hung gray over greasy rags. Standing still, he stared with nodding head at the dimly lit altar, then trudged on, his stick before him. A bustling verger snuffed the row of candles before a *pietà* and slipped past Otto into the sacristy, leaving a pleasing void behind him. From the organ droned one single long-held note: the organist must be arranging his music for the following service. The deep tone of the organ filled the church with vibration long after it had ceased to sound.

Otto drowsed off into a pleasant absence of thought. Nothing before or after this moment existed—no cares and difficulties, no expectations or desires. His two hands lay motionless on his knees against the gray woolen stuff of his trousers. Suddenly they became strange objects. They no longer formed part of himself. 'I shall fall asleep in a moment,' he thought—but no, that was not so: he saw things even more clearly than a moment ago. Slowly his eyes wandered across the nave.

And then he saw that Lili had come in and was walking down the center aisle; Lili, his own cousin Lili whom he had left a while back dead-tired after the doctor's visit. There she was walking, still rather shy, but erect, in spite of her threadbare summer cloak. In her arm she held a great sheaf of white lilies.

He repressed the impulse to jump up. Unconsciously he held his breath. He watched her walk on between the rows of chairs until she reached the altar. There she laid down her flowers upon the last step, crossed herself, and dropped onto her knees.

Otto dared not move. 'Thank God! Thank God!' something cried within him. She had ventured to do this; she had gone into the street alone, among people. He did not turn his eyes from her: and when he saw how fervently she bowed her head over her hands with the rosary, tears sprang into his eyes unawares —he felt this meant her salvation. In suspense, he followed her every movement closely, as one watches a sick child. He saw how her shoulders freed themselves, how they seemed to shake off an incubus, how she raised her head and threw it back, lost in the contemplation of the high altar with the miraculous image of Mary. He was completely engrossed in his close attention. He seemed to participate in every bowing of her head, every gesture of her praying hands. Time went by and he did not notice. In him something was praying with her: 'Help her, oh, help her—Maria hilf!'

Then he saw her get up and he crouched away in his pew; but she passed him with clear peaceful eyes that looked neither to the right nor to the left. Her footsteps trod lightly over the stone church floor. The little side door fell to behind her.

Like one who wakes, Otto heaved a deep sigh. He looked round. The church was still about him, but less empty. People were coming in for vespers. He stepped out of his pew. He looked at his watch again: five past seven. He must go at once to Roserl. But before leaving the church, he walked quickly to the steps of the altar, and bent over the flowers—it was as he had thought: he recognized his own lilies. From one of the stems hung a yellowed lettercard on which blazed the gilded Count's crown above Lili's monogram. On the card was written in her slender hand: "Maria hat geholfen!"

Otto was waiting with a throbbing heart outside the side entrance of Korngross's where the night porter assured him that Fräulein Goldös must still be upstairs. There she was, her little red hat tilted at a shade less provocative angle than at mid-day. Otto laughed as they met—she looked at him too seriously even for the new Roserl he had discovered that day.

Outside, he immediately put his arm through hers, oblivious of the group of young ladies who left the department store behind her. It did him good that she did not draw away. After that stupid telephone conversation he felt less confident than he had done that morning.

"You surely don't want to go strolling down the Luftbadgasse arm in arm with me?" asked Roserl at last. "It would damage our reputations, Otto."

"A fig for the Luftbadgasse," said Otto, and put his arm a little further through hers.

"Yes, but I've got to go on living there until my next increase in salary."

"You've become a real bourgeoise," said Otto reprovingly. "How shall I get that out of you again?"

"Don't concern yourself about that, boy. In a week's time it'll be nothing to you."

Otto was silent.

On the little square in front of the church Father Haydn kept watch as serenely as he had done three years ago. His smile still shone down very benevolently upon the couples who met there. As he passed by, Otto gave him a wink: how often had he stood there spying in the direction of Korngross's exit, and now he was walking in the clear light of day arm in arm, and with Roserl too, past the old gentleman. It was a great advance; and although he did not yet know where it would lead him, at that moment she gladdened him uncommonly. In the little passage beside the church, he could not help standing still and giving expression to his delight by suddenly kissing Roserl behind the left ear; and when she looked up at him, disconcerted and questioning, he said: "Sorry, darling, this is the first one in three years. I couldn't hold out any longer." He pressed her arm against his breast, and felt young, world-conqueringly young, full of still unknown but attainable possibilities.

"Stop," he said as they passed the Esterhazy park. "Let's see: it's twenty past seven. I've still five minutes to make arrangements with you for this evening. Come with me," and with his arm clinging tightly to hers he directed her faintly protesting steps inside the park gate.

"You're dragging me along as if I belonged to you legally," said Roserl.

"A fig for legality; you do belong to me," and Otto allowed his laughing, proud, tender gaze to sink deep into Roserl's eyes. "Just tell me if I can meet you here this evening at half-past nine."

"I thought you were booked this evening."

"I thought so too," said Otto, "but that's no longer the case. Darling, I really can't tell you everything in five minutes, can I? I thought I shouldn't be able to leave Aunt Paula and Lili alone for one moment this evening, and that I ought also to sleep at their place; but it's not as bad as that now—if I wish, I'm free at half-past nine. Then we can go where we like—if you like—Rosamündchen. Shall I wait for you here at half-past nine?"

The emotion that made him bring out these last words in an unusually hoarse and halting voice was bewildering, but incredibly joy-bringing. It was wonderful, incomprehensible, how all this could be so different from every previous experience. He swallowed, and clenched his teeth. He could not ask again: Roserl must answer.

He let go of her arm, and felt startled to find his knees were shaking. What was it? He had not known that happen before. Roserl had averted her face and stood motionless. He too stood alone. His arms hung limp. He waited, feeling this strange, uncontrollable trembling in his limbs, and his heart beating with deep, long beats.

"Your five minutes are up, Otto." It was supposed to sound funny, but when she looked at him her voice ran off into a whisper. "Ach du mein Gott. . . ." Then she folded her two hands round his arm. "I don't know—I'm no longer eighteen. I no longer know what I want; and yet I still love you so much— far too much. If I'm not here at half-past nine, you must leave me alone in future. Don't wait for me at the store any more—please."

A moment later the little red hat was bobbing down the steps to the Luftbadgasse. Otto, lost in thought, looked, smiling, towards the iron railing behind which it had descended into the void.

WHY did Roserl Goldös continue to live in the Luftbadgasse, when she could certainly have afforded a better abode than Frau Bergmann's bare front room, even though she did try to persuade herself that she could not? Well, simply because she had seen the two youngest Bergmann daughters born, and because she had been allowed to spoil all five children with many of such things as Korngross's stocked for that purpose. For a long time she had been regarded by all members of the family as a perpetual Father Christmas whom Providence had sent for their sakes to be domiciled in their front room. It was indeed a wise dispensation of the higher powers that enabled Roserl to supplement the necessaries of life for the family (since Bergmann, the head clerk, could hardly supply even them) by the addition of those little delights which alone give existence its full value. Frau Bergmann could have brought her sixth into the world without the new white-lacquered cradle with pink muslin curtains; but since Roserl had chosen that attractive show-piece at Korngross's for her, Frau Bergmann felt an extra satisfaction when, from the large double bed, she saw the small head of her youngest like a warm red fruit against the white pillowcase.

"Run downstairs now and wait for Roserl," said Frau Bergmann to her ten-year-old eldest daughter, who had just been allowed to come and see her new brother. "Tell her Grandmother has asked whether she will take supper downstairs, but see you don't miss her—otherwise she'll come up all these stairs for nothing." And thus it was that Roserl was received halfway up the Luftbadgasse by the youngest Resi, who threw two little arms around her knees and prevented her from going farther.

"Roserl, Roserl—we've received another child," said the little maid jubilantly, as she jumped up and down before Roserl's feet. She was a slender, dark little lassie, gifted with all the liveliness of her grandmother. "And at last it's a boy, you know—Grandfather says we've been a long time about it, but that it's turned out a real masterpiece."

"That's fine," said Roserl. "We'll go and look at once."

"But then you'll have to go up and down all those stairs, and Grandmother has asked whether you'll go and eat with the golden wedding party."

"Stuff and nonsense!" replied Roserl. "I must certainly first go and see the little brother lying in his new cradle."

"Yes, that's true, it's a picture. Even more beautiful than the Christ-child in Mariahilf."

"You see, it's something one ought to see," said Roserl. "You come along with me. Perhaps you'll be allowed to give it another little kiss too."

And so the big Roserl and the little Resi stepped arm in arm through the green-decked main gate, carefully crossed the empty entrance hall on tiptoe, passed quickly by the living-room where those who had stayed on were already sitting at table, and a moment later were tapping gently at the Bergmanns' bedroom door. The midwife peered cautiously round the corner, then she shook her head. "No, I can't do with children here," and little Resi sat down resignedly on the landing; but Roserl had already slipped through the door.

"Come quickly! Look!" said Frau Bergmann in the happy, tired voice of a healthy woman who had just been delivered. "There's no objection, is there?" and the friendly midwife, who was busy washing her hands, nodded consent.

Why did Roserl not seize Frau Bergmann's outstretched hand? Why did she in the first place bend over the little cradle where lay the newly born child? Frau Bergmann had a good idea why: Roserl was already twenty-six and mad about children.

"Isn't it handsome?" said the stout midwife, who, it goes without saying, bragged about every mite she swaddled, so long as it did not fall too far short of the minimum requirements. "The dearest little beak, and almost not red."

210

Ah, Roserl did not even notice whether the infant was a shade more or less red. This was the third she had seen born to Frau Bergmann, and each time it was a spectacle that moved her in the tenderest fibers of her womanhood. She did not pause to enquire the cause of her rapt absorption in every helpless little gesture of the tiny hands, in every small muscle contraction on the tender infant face; but when the minute red tongue unexpectedly ran quivering over the gleaming moist little lips, a warm tear that she wiped stealthily away rose to her eyes. She slipped her forefinger into the baby's tiny fist; and when she felt the contact of the suddenly clutching fingers a shiver ran through her limbs, and a second tear stood hot in the corners of her eyes. Roserl bent further over the cradle, and several warm drops fell upon the pink satin coverlet. The midwife noticed it. She said: "You have no children, Madame?"

Frau Bergmann hastened to answer: "The young lady is not married."

"I shouldn't have guessed that," stated the worldly-wise woman; and, true enough, Roserl was the very opposite of a languishing virgin. The midwife who, by virtue of her office, believed in the oneness of woman's body and mind, was convinced that Roserl had certainly not denied herself the urge towards the other sex. But also by virtue of her office, she thought it a pity that such a fresh, well-set-up young woman should deny her person its true destiny.

Meanwhile Roserl had stood up, and was wiping the side of her nose with a small silk handkerchief. The midwife winked, and with a wise little smile patted her shoulder.

"You should get married, young lady!" she said. "What do you young girls get out of all this variation? You can better rear the children of one man than put up with the whims and caprices of ten lovers."

"Sst!" expostulated Frau Bergmann. "It isn't as bad as that, is it, Roserl? The young lady is independent. She has a splendid job, and has no need to wait on anyone's caprices."

Roserl tried to make herself smile over the ten lovers; but deep in her heart she felt the thrust the words had given her. She knew: yes, that was it, precisely so. The amusing, sporting gad-about with whom she had spent a week-end not long ago in Baden had neither whims nor caprices, but neither was he a lover. He was, rather, a pleasant traveling companion with whom one also spent the night. The youngest under-manager at Korngross's, who in business was a pleasant, simple boy with whom it was possible to get on very well, became such an exacting lover on holiday that it was a relief to be able to resume the ordinary office relationship. Her most painful memory, however, was of that first gallant after Otto's sudden departure, at the time when she was trying to prove to herself that she could easily forget him: the young actor who, though on the boards he acted with charm and spontaneity, was in real life a sensual egoist and, when he made love, sank to his own natural level.

She sighed and thought: 'Yes, it's like that. A woman apparently can't have everything. Either she has work, well paid, interesting work that absorbs hands and mind—and in the periods when work does not absorb her sufficiently, a substitute in the way of human company—or she leads an existence like Frau Bergmann's with eternal care for every new day, but with the knowledge also that she is the center of the warm domesticity that springs up wherever a simple couple accept care as their inevitable heritage.'

Perhaps there was a third possibility; but a sensible woman was better advised not to think about that. Miracles did not happen in this world. Otto von Wernizek was in Vienna for six days. Then he would return to America; and Roserl Goldös was determined she would not cry again as she had cried three years ago—one did that only once in a lifetime.

A little wail, soft and high-pitched, movingly human, rose from the cradle. Roserl bent over it again. Under the cradle curtain hung the soft, lukewarm emanation of a freshly bathed infant's body with the spicy, fernlike aroma of the pillow that had grown warm. She ran her forefinger softly over the delicate curve of the baby's cheek: how perfect, how unutterably, how wonderfully perfect was all this, suddenly present like a gift.

"Come," said the midwife, "now we must help Madame." She threw back the bedclothes, and looked round to see whether Roserl was going.

Roserl ought to have gone, but it was a question whether she could go. At that moment as never before, the somber mystery of generation gripped her by the throat. Oh, no, a child was no gift. The room was suddenly changed. It was no longer the blithe, bright environment of a sleeping infant who lay there as if it had been caught up from heaven into its little white cradle: it was the lying-in room, the place where, in pain, a new human being had been born. From under the raised bedclothes came a penetrating, almost animal exhalation—blood and sweat had done their work there. There was suffering and toil, there muscles had twisted and brought forth, in compliance with the blind omnipotence of nature that impelled them to the one eventual end. The odor of passionate exertion still hung heavy above the lying-in bed, over which the midwife bent devotedly.

And yet it was only Frau Bergmann who lay there, the simple mother of six children, the unpretentious bedfellow of pale-faced Herr Bergmann who fulfilled with such care his duties as head clerk. Thousands of women daily lay prostrate in the same way, prepared to endure what had to be endured. It was the commonest of happenings, a very normal, statistically registered phenomenon. Why then did Roserl take the limp hand of Frau Bergmann in hers with such boundless respect? Why did she feel unable to leave this room where the smell of stimulated human organs pervaded the air; why did she feel herself riveted to the spot where the dark forces moving her too expressed themselves in their full potency?

She was no longer aware that she stood there, a very indiscreet intruder in the lying-in room. She saw the broad bent back of the midwife, saw the sturdy legs planted on the bedclothes, saw the quiet care with which her hands did their work. It was all necessary. Nothing happened here for pleasure or convention. And suddenly she gripped herself. Her hands glided down her body, over her silk jumper and her well-fitting skirt, over her firm rounded breasts, her slender, sturdy thighs. God, how empty and hollow she was with her unused organs, her well-tended exterior within which nothing was allowed to grow.

Frau Bergmann groaned a little. She apologized: really it was nothing—perhaps just some after-pains.

"May I have the little one in bed?" she asked the midwife, who was about to wash her hands again.

"Why, yes," said she. "Just let the Fräulein bring you the child." And then gently, very, very gently, Roserl lifted the little warm heap out of the cradle and laid it in its mother's arm. Frau Bergmann's cheek, yellow pale and old, contrasted with the pink bloom of the infant's skin, but the movement with which she received it, that self-assuring gesture of possession and protection, was not old: it was eternally young, the all-embracing movement of the determined mother animal, and of the tender human mother combined.

Roserl turned away. She must go—what was the good of watching this and pretending that she rejoiced at the joy of a mother? What was the good of it all; even if later on she could occasionally borrow the child for an hour or so, and put on its baby clothes and jingle a rattle at it? Those were little games for idle moments. At that moment Roserl saw her generosity, her offering of little presents and luxury clothes, precisely for what it was: a pose, a disguise for her actual heart's desire to have children like Frau Bergmann, real children of flesh and blood; to bear them, to enclose them in her arms, to feed them from herself, hour after hour; and at night when everyone was asleep to lie listening for the little sounds that came from them, and to give them what they wanted.

"Tomorrow morning he may try to drink," promised the midwife, "tonight make your husband give him a little spoonful of tepid water," and these plain commonplace words surrounded the Bergmann couple in Roserl's heart with an atmosphere of tenderness. Yes, it would be like that, of course—the woman would hear the child's soft little moan. Carefully she would nudge the sleeping man, dazed after a day of exhausting, tedious work; but all the same he would get up very willingly and, standing in his crumpled nightshirt, he would warm the little spoon of water and then let it carefully flow into the tiny mouth. By the night-light, the woman would see it happen. She would smile. . . .

"I'm going down now," said Roserl. She was finding it too hard to remain calm and cheerful on this lying-in visit. Hastily she went towards the door, then turned back for a second to press into the midwife's hand the two-schilling piece that was her due.

Of course Roserl could not go downstairs into the turmoil of the golden wedding party, from which rose buzzing noise in waves. She would get something to eat later on, when she went to the coffee-house to read her paper: she would ask for a couple of rolls with her coffee. And then she forgot all about the possibility that she was hungry. She sat before the little dressing-table in her room and looked at herself in the glass with large fixed eyes; but cry she would not. The vertical furrow in her forehead made a commanding exclamation-point between her brows.

Then cautious footsteps crossed the landing. The door of the bedroom turned on its hinges, and through the wall Roserl heard Frau Bergmann's friendly voice replying softly to a subdued question from Herr Bergmann. The face in the mirror suddenly looked back at her with a disquietingly strained expression. Then she seized her handbag and her little hat and fled out into the Luftbadgasse.

. . . .

At a quarter past nine the sky was still a wide expanse of blazing opal above the treetops of the Esterhazy park; and although the yellow lamps shone against the foliage until it hung there like a gold-green stage set, nobody on this mellow summer evening was prepared to admit that night was about to begin. Roserl only brought the silk chemise she was embroidering a little closer to her eyes and went on working with regular, skillful, sweeping movements. She had been there since half-past eight. In the coffee-house a group of actors from the Theater an der Wien, celebrating some occasion, had been short of ladies. Usually Roserl knew how to decline such invitations with a joke, but tonight she had to get up. She could not bear the coffee-house. So now she was after all sitting in the Esterhazy park, but not by the gate where Otto von Wernizek was to meet her. She had discovered a little place of her own in this much frequented city park, and was sitting on the small folding chair she had borrowed from the lady at the kiosk, almost completely concealed among a group of low acacias. It was a precarious place for a young woman who wanted to prepare herself for a sensible conversation, for the waves of honey-sweet stupor that streamed out of the acacias were wafted from a world that had no single link with the human capacity for reasoning; but Roserl had imprudently chosen this fragrant corner because from there she had a view of the park gate without herself being visible.

As a matter of fact, it was unnecessary for her to have a talk with Otto, because she was now certain that she would not go out with him, neither this evening nor any other evening. But she wanted to tell him why. She did not want just to stay away—to let him stand and wait till perhaps late in the evening. That would be impossible: after all, he apparently still loved her a little. Thus she sat in her beflowered observation-post, waiting till she saw him. It would be easier to meet him if she had previously seen him approach, if she had already taken in his step, his bearing, his animated face—she remembered her weakness of the morning when he had stood suddenly before her.

But he did not come. Her hands with the flimsy silk garment had been lying idle in her lap for some time. The clock had struck half-past nine quite ten minutes ago, and still he was not in sight. Roserl took a deep breath—it really was a good thing she had not been waiting at the park gate; but all the same her heart was dully oppressed with disappointment. She had never anticipated such remissness. The weight of all she wanted to say to him, to explain to him so that he should understand and exonerate her, she must now carry unuttered within herself. It was very difficult to get up and go home, almost impossible to return to her bedroom near the lying-in room with the contented mother and her child.

At ten o'clock it was almost dark; she had already

put away her embroidery in her handbag. She got up: in any case she could no longer see as far as the entrance to the park. She clapped-to the little folding chair and stood in the twilight, quite alone and lost in the clump of acacias that breathed out the unendurable sweetness of their luxuriant blossom. Then, like a punished school-child, with hanging head she laid the borrowed stool against the long-closed kiosk and walked slowly towards the exit.

In the Scheidekgasse stood an attractive gray two-seater alongside the park railing: yes, it was an evening to go driving into the Wienerwald in such a fast, smooth-running car. Roserl pressed her lips tightly together—there was nobody to go out driving with anyhow. Perhaps when Korngross's gave her the power to sign, she would treat herself to a cheap little car. . . .

And then she was seized roughly by the arm. Otto's darkened eyes looked down upon her.

"You naughty girl! Is it right to leave me waiting here like this? I suppose you've been sitting watching all this time to see if I had the blues enough?"

"Where have you come from?" asked Roserl, startled.

"Where have *you* come from?" asked Otto, raising his voice.

"I was sitting over there in the park," said Roserl, "waiting to see you come. I wanted to talk to you. But where were you?"

"I was sitting here in this little car, and did not take my eyes off the park gate a moment. I was here at a quarter past nine. I was able to hire this thing until tomorrow, and I thought: 'If she comes, I'll take her with me to the Wienerwald.'"

"Otto," said Roserl, imploringly, "I must talk to you."

"Yes," said Otto, "we know all about that—talk, wasting the precious time talking, you women always want to do that—but you used not to be like that. Perhaps you wanted to receive my confession there in that little garden?"

"Otto," said Roserl, "you must first listen to me—"

"No," answered Otto, at last letting go of her arm which he had held all this time in an almost painful grip. "No, I don't want to listen to you. Either you come along with me, now at once and without palaver —or you'll go your own way home. You can't leave a man waiting until he's eaten up his nails and then expect him to hold a conference with you on the meaning of life. Either you still love me enough to want what I want; or we'll bid each other good-by and you'll go quietly home. . . . But why in God's name did you come here in that case?"

Roserl was asking herself: 'Why did I come?' but simultaneously she knew the answer: 'Because I could not stay away.' Thus it was, and it was no use wanting to know why—it had nothing to do with knowledge.

She gave a soft, dry little sob and rubbed her forehead against Otto's arm, lost as a little stray dog.

"Come," said he, and laid his arm about her shoulders, "come," and helped her into the car.

OF COURSE Paul Wolùk played the piano—even a little better than one might have expected of a violinist. Maria had not been mistaken. How she had succeeded in getting the boy out of his pavilion was not very clear even to her. Naturally she saw nothing out of the ordinary in a spontaneous artists' friendship of the kind that is daily formed and broken in every artists' circle in the world; but that this shy youth had submissively allowed himself to be carried off without a word of protest when she went to fetch him was nothing short of a miracle. She did not know that the white cat had been lying kittening under Paul's divan ever since six o'clock in the afternoon.

It was past ten, and since eight o'clock the wedding party had been rising to its climax. The Chinese lanterns cast just enough exotic light over the green garlands to transform the entrance hall into an intimate festival chamber where they had no need to discern one another to know that they were all present together: the festive atmosphere bound the hundred-headed family into a vaguely conscious, indivisible whole. Thrills of emotion and pleasure communicated themselves unhindered from person to person. They

223

nodded to one another. Sometimes, from sheer delight, one of them rubbed against his nearest neighbor, and then brushed away a tear, careless of whether his gesture was observed. The festival belonged to them all. Everyone co-operated in it and gave of his best. Father and Mother Hodl, of course, constituted the central point; and everyone could see their pleasure: like a royal pair, they sat on their decorated chairs upon a platform decked out with bunting that was really not too rickety to support them. It stood in the center of the long side wall of the entrance hall. They had a full view of everything and everybody, and the grandchildren who came to recite their little verses or sing appropriate songs were raised before their audience upon this eminence. The young people were going through many an anxious moment. In a corner next to the platform the little victims were huddled together. "Your turn still to come? Your turn still to come?"—But when they stood before their audience, helped on with little encouraging nods, they spouted forth their poetical contributions as if there was no such thing as stage-fright. When it was over, they received a kiss from their grandmother, and from Johannes Hodl a twenty groschen piece with which to buy an ice. Yes, that was another attraction—an unemployed neighbor with an ice-cream barrow had received permission to ply his trade by the main gate. When the dancing began he would certainly earn a pretty penny; besides, Hodl really could not go on providing the whole neighborhood with light refreshments.

For the Luftbadgasse was joining merrily in the festival. Not the reduced gentry, of course, who were ashamed of inhabiting this neighborhood, but the small shopkeepers and all those who accepted a pleasant moment without pausing to ask its source. Outside the wide-open main gate feet were already on the move with every number played by the house orchestra; but the real dancing had not begun yet— that would not come until the first part of the program was over. Maria Ritter had been heard in breathless silence: this audience did not trouble about a shaky note or unsatisfactory breath control; they appreciated to the full the gusto with which the old lady sang her beloved arias. There were connoisseurs among them who had heard her in her prime. When they closed their eyes, they did not notice such a very great difference; they listened to their beautiful memories, and applauded enthusiastically from gratitude. It was no small matter either that Maria should be singing there in their midst: Maria Ritter, who was celebrating with the whole neighborhood like any ordinary person.

And Maria too was happy, once more perfectly and indescribably happy. It was years since she had enjoyed this devout attention that hung upon her, attention to which she could give all that was in her; and

225

when after Rosine's great aria the applause simply refused to die down, and when she as in the old days after her greatest triumphs remained standing, her arms outstretched to signify that this was too much for her, that she herself felt moved to tears of gratitude—then enthusiasm gripped the Luftbadgasse, and shouting seemed as though it would have no end until Johannes junior, the tacitly accepted Master of Ceremonies, hoisted little Resi once more onto the platform. She was Herr Bergmann's eldest, and calm descended upon them again as they listened indulgently to the childish voice that, after Maria's performance, sounded like the artless bleating of a dear little lamb.

Herr Bergmann had written some lines to the tune of the *Kaiserlied*, to which his heart was still pledged (at the time he had been rejected for active service). He was particularly proud of his last verse, which had cost him much cudgeling of the brain. Little Resi sang it a shade out of tune, but with childlike conviction:

> "Dear people, may God spare you
> Full many and many a year
> For we today here fête you,
> An exemplary golden pair.
> And when from out the earthly throng
> You take at last your way
> May Heaven receive you with a song,
> Joyful as this present day."

Grandmother Resi brushed away a tear. She was very sensitive to allusions to an unknown hereafter that, after all, each day brought a day nearer; but old Hodl smiled. Why, yes, why should not Heaven, which he thought he would reach as quickly as possible after the inevitable purgatory, be as pleasant as this fine day in this acceptable world? It was not at all a bad idea either that there above one should celebrate an eternal golden wedding with all one's beloved relatives whom one had seen depart during this life, or would soon have to leave behind; with our good Lord looking in now and again, as the parish priest had done that afternoon. He gave an extra clap for little Resi, and shook his blushing son-in-law heartily by the hand.

Maria Ritter had listened to the song with only half an ear: so many children had sung to her before; and besides, she was still completely overcome by the shattering emotion aroused in her by renewed contact with a listening audience. Her being was filled with a vast, stimulating joy. Stealthily she glanced at Paul Woluk, who with absent eyes sat staring at the keyboard, completely lost to all that was happening round him. In her overflowing feeling of sympathy, she felt a deep desire that this self-centered boy also should experience something of the joys of the performing artist. She descended from the platform, laid her hand upon his arm, and said: "Paul, go and fetch your violin and play something to them."

"What made you think of that?" asked Paul. Maria felt him shrink into himself, and her hand glided as far as his hand that was playing soft little runs on the highest notes. The hand lay still at once. Then she withdrew hers.

"Because you would give them so much pleasure. God, boy, if I with my old bass can persuade them to listen, what couldn't you do for them!"

"I don't want to do anything for them," growled Paul Woluk. "I accompanied a little to please you, but I'm packing up now."

"No, you mustn't," cried Maria. "You've got to accompany me again a little later. In some Schubert songs." She had no intention of letting him go, for then she would certainly not see him again that evening. A sly little smile glided over her lips. She beckoned to Josephine. Yes, that was an idea. She would have his violin fetched without asking him again. His violin must be lying somewhere within reach in his room. With motherly devotion, she looked down on his head again, as it bent once more over the keyboard. A moment later, she resumed her place on the platform.

And now the house orchestra wanted to give a turn. The boys played the "Schöne blaue Donau." True, they did so for the third time, but that did not matter. It was the piece they played best, and they rocked backwards and forwards to it with conviction.

Outside on the pavement people were dancing

openly. Few paid attention to two somberly clad men who stepped out of a car and worked their way through the crush until they reached the back stairs, which they ascended without looking round. They had exchanged a few words with Franzl, who had run to attend particularly to the burning Chinese lanterns; that was all.

Five minutes later they came downstairs again. They had apparently been to the Jonathans', for Daniel was walking between them.

At the same moment, Josephine appeared with the abducted violin case. She pressed forward behind the men until she reached the platform; but there she stood stock-still, staring with large eyes at the strangers who, with Daniel Jonathan, were forcing their way through the entrance hall. "Save us!" whispered Josephine, as she pulled at Maria Ritter's skirt.

Maria bent down. "What is it?"

"Someone's been run in," stammered Josephine, "that Jew boy on the third floor."

"You're mad, woman," said Maria, laughing. "You must be wrong. Where do you get that idea?"

"Sst!" murmured Josephine, and her anxious face suddenly extinguished Maria's gaiety. "I saw it myself. Just look: one's walking in front and the other behind. You can't see his hands from here, but I saw them when I was walking behind them—he's handcuffed."

"Jesu Maria," whispered the old lady, "what's

going to happen next?" and peered into the reddish glow of the entrance hall. Several others appeared to have noticed something too. There was restrained excitement in the group that pressed forward with Johannes junior towards the door through which the three men had disappeared. The unsuspecting orchestra went on playing full of *animo,* and old Hodl beat time fierily with his foot: it was his favorite waltz—he had danced it on his first wedding day.

"The Blue Danube" flowed cheerfully on, but the couples who had been happily turning on the pavement outside the main gate came to a standstill. The orchestra reached the final chords and smiled expectantly; but the applause was thin. Only near the platform did it break out spontaneously.

Suddenly Maria stood up beside Herr Hodl's chair. "A moment's attention, ladies and gentlemen!" People looked up and about them. "Now our master violinist, Herr Paul Wolùk, is going to give us a treat. Herr Wolùk, may I beg you?"

Paul looked up from the piano. From the platform Maria beckoned, and Paul shrugged his shoulders. But he did not know Maria Ritter, Maria who when fire broke out at the opera in Madrid went on singing while the scenery was being deluged with water. "Here's your violin!" cried Maria, and waved Paul's instrument, which, though it would never obtain a certificate, was as dear to him as if it had been a Stradivarius.

"Are you possessed?" cried Paul, as he jumped onto the platform. "Keep your fingers off it!" He seized the violin from her hands; and good-natured applause rose at once from those sitting near the platform. Maria smiled triumphantly: he was trapped.

Taken by surprise, Paul Wolùk looked round and saw there was no escape. Father Hodl nodded gratefully to him. The bride was already sitting trimly upright, smoothing out her silk skirt. The audience assumed an expectant attitude as it exchanged nods of satisfaction: the Hodls were certainly offering them a very special treat. It was true that by the main gate there stood a gesticulating group around Johannes junior, who had to request silence with special emphasis; but that was no reason for not beginning at once.

"Play, Wolùk," whispered Maria, "play, man. I'll tell you why later on."

"What in God's name must I play?" asked Paul, and laid his pocket handkerchief firmly against his neck.

"It doesn't matter what—for all I care play the *Haidenröslein*—anything, provided you play."

"Here goes, then," said Paul, submitting, "but I'll make you pay for it, Frau Direktor."

And now Paul played for the very first time in his life to complete strangers in a completely unknown place, and played as well as he thought he could play only in his own room. It was not in the least like the

231

compulsory pupils' concerts at the Graz School of Music, where he had known individually every one of the listeners and could identify them with all their human failings and unpleasantnesses; neither were there any teachers here who would afterwards condescendingly rub in their own impotence. Here there was only a shadowy space full of simple people, among whom, however, there were more music lovers than in any other city in the world.

Paul Wolùk had begun with the *Haidenröslein,* and why not? He improvised some attractive variations as he played. The audience nodded and smiled —this was delightful. They did not seem to have had enough yet. He tried something more classical; it would be an amusing experiment to see how far he could carry them along with him. Corelli's little sonata earned warm appreciation. Then he ventured upon Bach. The boys of the mandolin orchestra listened with bowed heads: this was music, and Maria Ritter's heart was jubilant. Maria's childish heart rejoiced and forgot quickly: she had entirely forgotten Daniel Jonathan. So had the others. Rows of faces stared inside through the main gate. Grateful applause came in from far up the listening Luftbadgasse.

And then Paul Wolùk laid his violin closer to his chin, closed his eyes, and played Mozart, his Mozart, whom he had loved from the moment his first teacher had allowed him to play the first sonatina phrase. He had been true to this love; it had even stood the test of the arranged "Klassische Stücke" which he had had to play because Mozart was thought so "childish." Childish? Yes, as the innocent children around God's throne are childish. Bereft of all weight, rising and falling, shining with heavenly light. Paul Wolùk played the Adagio from the A sharp concerto. But not for his audience—not even for himself: he played because the music would flow on, would pour itself out from note to note.

Maria Ritter was not embarrassed by the fact that she was crying for joy. She let her tears flow, smiling with wet cheeks, and thought neither of handkerchief nor powder-puff. This was really and truly music. She saw the many happy faces about her, and felt comforted at the thought that so long as such music existed and people could play like that, her beloved world could not perish.

Paul Wolùk opened his eyes. His cheek released the violin. Applause broke out, swelled in volume, grew into a storm of passionate utterance. Maria seized the hand that held the bow, and Father Hodl began gratefully to explain how impressive he had found it. But by this time Paul Wolùk had returned to reality. He looked across the throng of uproarious citizens. Where was he? What was he doing here? A painful shudder swept across his pale face; then he knitted his brows. Hastily he put his violin in its case and sprang sideways from the platform.

"Let them thank you, foolish boy!" cried Maria

after him; but he pushed his way through the still loudly applauding audience.

Then suddenly he stood before an immovable object: a tall man of unmistakable Yankee type thrust his smiling person against Paul, brought both hands down upon his shoulders, and cried with conviction: "That was fine, my boy. You made quite a hit. What's your name?"

It was Mr. Haymaker who, in spite of himself, had been dragged thither by his friend Hunter, and had been standing for the last quarter of an hour listening by the main gate while his companion went up to the Wernizeks' flat. He was genuinely enthusiastic: despite his commercial appearance he could appreciate art. Besides, his practical mind had at once made a comparison between the playing of this lad and that of his expensive Italian first violin.

"Where are you going?" asked Haymaker, for like an insect whose way is obstructed Paul had with renewed energy taken the opposite direction. But after three steps, he found himself again confronted by the still more energetic Haymaker.

"Don't be a fool," said he, still smiling cheerily. But Paul swore inwardly and planted his elbow so positively in Haymaker's stomach that the American gasped for breath, and Paul seized the opportunity to disappear through the back door into his dark, gravestone-filled wilderness. Nobody but himself could traverse that by night without getting covered in

234

bruises. "Get out, I hope you choke, the lot of you!" he wished half aloud. Then, lifting his knees, he picked his way back to the pavilion, and found the white cat installed upon a sheet of music paper with four small tabby kittens that she had licked clean. She miaowed a welcome, and he immediately poured his milk supply onto a plate; after which he kicked off his shoes and closely inspected the bristling wet infants.

A pale little lady of indefinite age had informed Mr. Hunter in correct English that Count Wernizek was not at home, and would certainly not return that evening, and that she did not know where he had gone. Mr. Hunter was shocked—what was the fellow doing that he should lie about it?—and in his heart he was very envious of Otto who knew his way about in Vienna.

When he got downstairs after his lengthy interrogation, he found Haymaker in conference with the aged singer to whom he had been introduced that afternoon.

"Come along, Haymaker," said Mr. Hunter, completely ignoring Maria's presence. "Your friend isn't at home—he's actually on the go this very first evening."

"Shut up!" commanded Haymaker, and became engrossed anew in his conversation.

"I don't mind trying," said Maria finally, "but I should advise you to wait till tomorrow."

"But, my dear lady, I'm booked all day tomorrow. I'm an official, and have to attend this competition. Oh, you know what I mean, in the Konzerthaus."

Maria smiled. She knew indeed what he meant. Not content with the beauty competition of the Vienna mannequins, the festival week committee was bringing musicians from all countries into the lists against one another. The previous year a Polish pianist and a Salzburg violinist had won the prize; and they had never been heard of again.

"On your own responsibility then," said Maria, "but we shall have to take a light in order to reach him—otherwise we shall break our necks."

"All right," and Haymaker carefully broke off from the decorations a fir twig bearing a Chinese lantern. Franzl did not even notice; the ball was now in full swing, and he too wanted to dance a turn with his appetizing little wife.

"Forward, then," said Maria, and led the way through the back door. Hunter, who did not want to lose sight of his friend, joined them. He found it only moderately agreeable on this dark evening to go feeling his way about a spot that he could not help taking for a deserted churchyard. But he had thrown himself into the stream when he left Midland, and allowed himself in silence and with stoic cynicism to be conveyed to the place where he would be washed ashore.

Paul Woluk had of course heard that there were intruders in his domain. Three people could not walk over that very uneven surface noiselessly. With a great effort, he turned the rusty key of the little pavilion door, and spied at them as they approached through the window. "Madame Butterfly," he smirked, as he watched the ample Maria, with a lantern in one hand and her lifted skirt in the other, jumping over the gravestones, and was greatly amused by his own wit. Oh, yes, Paul Woluk certainly found himself the best company.

Maria pushed against the little door. Of course it was closed; she had expected nothing else. She raised the wrought-iron knocker that squeaked and groaned unmelodiously. Then she let it fall. The unexpectedly loud sound vibrated through the little house and even frightened her. She raised her eyebrows and looked at Mr. Haymaker dubiously. But he nodded contentedly: that sound would raise the dead, and certainly therefore a young musician.

The door was not opened, however. Haymaker let the knocker fall a second time, even more forcefully than Maria had done. After which, something inside seemed to be knocked down. But the door remained closed. Haymaker shrugged his shoulders and went to examine the windows.

Inside, Paul Woluk was standing before his washstand trying with trembling fingers to stop his ears with little pieces of sponge. He was determined to

237

evade the calamity that was descending upon him: if they were going to batter in his abode, he would lie like a log; they should not get a word out of him; and as a consoling prospect he promised himself that in the morning his first business would be to look out for a new abode—surely there was to be found somewhere in Vienna a place where he would not meet fellow musicians—even if it had to be a nudist colony. He remained standing in front of his washstand even when the little house shook again and again under the hand of Mr. Hunter, who had not made up his mind to go to bed.

Meanwhile, Mr. Haymaker tapped several times on the windows, and that did strike Maria as being too bad.

"Come," she said, "you see we have no success. Let's go back." She was feeling very guilty, but Haymaker, who was not the boss of an American symphony orchestra for nothing, could not allow this affront to his consciousness of power. Hell, when he had the luck to discover a good violinist, he was not going to take it lying down like this; and so he knocked on the pane energetically. But Mr. Hunter, who had had more than enough of this waiting about, had a better plan: he twisted his penknife under the most rickety of the catches and succeeded quite easily in lifting it out of the old wood. Now it was only a small matter to lift the window. Mr. Haymaker was already pushing his head forward into the breach thus

238

made, when Paul, at his wit's end, seized his wash-basin and hurled the contents venomously towards the window.

Mr. Haymaker drew back. This was the limit. There are few things before which an American re-treats; but before a wave of malodorous washing-water from a Vienna backyard, a convinced hygienist may give ground with honor. And so he shook his drenched coat, wiped his head and hair with two pocket handkerchiefs, seized the Chinese lantern from Maria's hands, and began the retreat.

"Auf wiedersehen," said Maria politely when at last the three of them were standing in the Luft-badgasse. "Shall I see you again one of these days?"

"Depend upon it," barked Haymaker. "Tomorrow I shall be lying in the hospital with a pestilential in-fection. But even if I remain healthy—they can keep this violinist of yours in Vienna. I'm not having a maniac in my orchestra, even though he were the greatest artist in the world."

"I feared as much," said Maria. "You come from Midland, don't you?"

Haymaker gave her a searching glance, but in view of the fact that he could not brawl with a lady, he bowed hastily and turned away with Mr. Hunter, who did not even take off his hat.

"If only they bruise their shins on the steps," said Maria vengefully. But then for quite five minutes she stood still in the mellow evening, and looked up

239

towards the starry sky that was visible even out of this crevice in the town. Stars are very high and very unattainable. Maria felt small. When she had looked up long enough, the remarkable thought occurred to her: 'Perhaps Paul Wolùk is right after all.'

ABOVE the Wienerwald, too, the stars lay high and unattainable; but those who left the main road and penetrated along the narrow rising paths between the trees lost sight of the stars. They walked over thick soft moss in the damp breath of the wood, under a low-hanging roof of leaves that shut off the earth from heaven.

Otto had laid his arm about Roserl's waist and was helping her up the incline. He penetrated deeper and deeper into the dark, still, warm wood whose fragrance stimulated him headily. He would certainly not have dared to bring another woman with him on such a gypsy adventure; but with Roserl everything was allowed. "Is it soft enough here, child?" he asked, when he found on the ground a soft carpet of fern that gave under the foot. He could not see her. He could only guess at her. He knelt down by her and groped towards her with quivering hands. "Do you want me still? Are you still mine?—answer me, darling." But there was no other answer except her two arms laid firmly about his neck, holding down his head. He sighed deeply—almost painfully deeply; let himself go—and was home, finally, finally home.

. . . .

"Are you crying, dearest?"

There was no reply. With the flat of his hand, Otto stroked her eyes. The hand grew moist. "Why do you cry? Everything was all right?"

"Everything is still all right," said Roserl—it was no love lie: she was happy, unspeakably happy, so filled and gratefully satisfied that her eyes grew moist with the overwhelming bliss. "Perhaps I was crying because this cannot go on," said Roserl, and laid Otto's hand closer to her breast. She clung tightly to his warmth and whispered: "Don't be angry with me because I say that. I didn't think of it at the time, but now I know it again."

"Where is it then?" asked Otto. "Come here, little one. I'll kiss it away again." His mouth sought her mouth, his arms enfolded her again with tender violence, until her body relaxed against him, and he felt that she need think no more.

How trusting and innocent grows the human body that dares to abandon itself in order to become one with another: so innocent that, like a child's, it can sink from the highest bliss into defenseless joint sleep. The woman came to herself first. She awoke from a wonderfully joyous dream into an even deeper gladness of reality: against her shoulder lay his head, cradled in her arm in such complete surrender to rest that she could continue to dream at his side. She lay thus a long time, listening to his breathing, completely absorbed in the all-pervading joy of his nearness. More deeply, more sweetly than ever before, she experienced the presence of her lover. Motionless, she enjoyed every slight movement of his limbs as they rested against her. Round her, the little woodland sounds wove a lively net over the deep stillness of the night, and she smiled as she thought of the small invisible lives that stirred among the rustling leaves and under the carpet of moss. A late nightingale sent a single quivering note through the darkness; the note remained languishing, seeking, unanswered. Then in the distance a throaty glugging gave reply. Roserl's smile deepened in the swelling richness of that perfect hour.

Then the moon rose and scattered a tremulous sheen among the branches. A gleam of light touched the sleeping man. He opened his eyes and looked into the warmly tinted face of the young woman beside him. Her eyes had still the dark glow he had awakened there. The impulse to take to himself once more her beneficent womanhood ebbed away again. He reached upwards and took her head between his hands.

"Only now do I see you properly, Rosamündchen. How do you come to be so lovely?"

Roserl shrugged one shoulder. She did not want to talk; but Otto, who was following with his finger the line of her small delicate ear down to the soft lobe, went on: "Do you know you're prettier than all the countesses put together? And you haven't even blue blood in your veins!"

"That's all you know," said Roserl, and laid her hand over his, which gave in and lay still. "My great grandmother was a serf, and my grandfather was as handsome and erect as the old baron. I knew them both. No, boy, there's much more blue blood in the world than you think—and that's why I haven't as much respect for it as you have."

"I've no respect for it," said Otto, defending himself. "I only think it imposes certain obligations— oh, don't let's talk nonsense, Rosamündchen. I can't help it that I have it. Give me another kiss, darling, and let's try to find shelter somewhere."

They had left the edge of the wood. The dark rustling treetops lay behind them. Before them a little winding pathway led downwards between fields. A short distance away on one side gleamed a fire, and the moonlight shone upon several white patches.

"Campers?" asked Roserl.

"We'll go and see," said Otto. It was in his nature never to pass anything attractive if he had the time to examine it at his ease.

The campers proved to be students—six young people of diverse nationality who were studying in Vienna, but had an unexpected holiday owing to the compulsory closing of the university. They did not want to have anything to do with students' riots, and were therefore camping while they waited for more normal times to return. There were Italians,

244

an Argentine, a Negro, a tall Norwegian, and, actually, a Chinese: with precious little gestures, he unfolded a stool for Roserl who, interested, stood looking at the campfire.

"You play too," said Otto, pointing to the Negro's banjo.

"Yes," said the Norwegian, "didn't you hear us a little while ago? We've sung through our whole repertory."

Otto smiled at Roserl. "Strange! No, we didn't hear anything; but we should like to stay and listen a while. It's too warm to go in yet."

"Oh, yes; folk-songs," said Roserl.

"Fire away then!" commanded the Norwegian. He was obviously enthusiastic over Roserl's presence. They sang in turn: the melancholy nasal sound of the little Chinese followed by the really fine tenor of one of the Italians. Then the Norwegian sang several peasant ditties, and as he sang he danced with vigorous jumps and knee-bendings. Those who could sang with him. It was really very attractive: but then Otto remembered that the two-seater he had borrowed was still parked somewhere below without supervision.

"We must be getting home," said he, and got up from the circle in front of the tent. "Many thanks, gentlemen!"

"No, don't go yet," said the Norwegian, "you haven't heard our best number yet. The lady mustn't miss that for anything. Come on, Johnny; it's your turn now."

The Negro, who had been squatting silent and pensive by the fire, put his banjo submissively between his knees and played an opening bar. The hesitant thrumming sounded thin and melancholy in the little field. Then, in a tender, rather hoarse baritone, he sang the long-drawn-out, wonderfully melodious airs about which Otto had never understood why they had come to be called spirituals.

'That's out of the picture here,' thought Roserl, 'that doesn't belong to a field with marguerites and moonshine. That belongs to water, a wide expanse of water.' And then the boy did sing the song of the Swanee River. At first several of the others sang with him. Then one by one the strange voices fell silent: they did not blend; their sound did not mix with the other sound. Only that deep, rather husky voice could sing the negro songs: it felt its way, full of melancholy, through hummed refrains, and strung together verse after verse, song after song into one long somber string. "All de world am sad and dreary," wailed the voice—without growing sentimental. It wailed because it must, because it longed for something lost. Thus does a dog wail imprisoned in its kennel. It was heartbreaking to hear this black boy, dressed like a European in polo shirt and plus fours, singing by the flickering campfire of his nostalgic longing for the old plantation which had been his home.

246

"This is a mad world," said Otto, when, with Roserl on his arm, he at last continued the descent along the meandering path towards the Fahrstrasse. "Here's this nigger in a foreign continent wishing himself back among his own people: and in a few weeks I shall be on the other side, longing for this same little field where he feels so melancholy. Everything's absolutely topsy-turvy, Rosamündchen. We've played musical chairs, and have all run from our places at the same time. There's really only one place in the whole world for me—close to you, darling."

THE spotlight in front of the Schloss-hotel Cobenzl was suddenly switched on again, although the hall clock had already struck twelve in its singsong Westminster melody. The night porter hurried to the steps, and saw from a discreet distance a very attractive young woman being lifted from a trim little two-seater by a tall cavalier. When the young woman had been set down carefully, he rushed forward to take the luggage.

"No luggage," said Otto von Wernizek.

The porter raised an eyebrow. "What do you want, sir?"

"A good room at the front."

The porter raised a second very dubious eyebrow. "Impossible, sir. Full up! The Rotary Congress, sir."

"Oh? Do the Americans take precedence these days?" asked Otto, rising to his full aristocratic height. The porter appraised him with a pensive eye. He thought there was a good chance that this fellow-countryman, obviously in luck's way, would be generous. He walked into the hall and Otto followed him.

"What name, sir?" he asked, pushing forward the guest book.

"Let me have it," said Otto, and wrote in his most

typical upright hand: 'Otto von Wernizek-Bolnanyi and wife.'

The pale night porter bowed almost double; now that the guest had entered his name in that way, he was sure of his tip, luggage or no luggage. "Perhaps I have a room on the front after all, Herr Graf. I'll have another look."

"Why, yes, just have another look," said Otto. "I'll run the car into the garage."

When he returned, Roserl was waiting on one of the hall benches. She sat so lost in thought that she did not even hear him come. He slipped his arm under hers, and drew her to her feet. Like all men, he wanted first place in the interest of the woman who was with him. Arm in arm with her, he crossed the hall; but then she stood still and pointed to the guest book. "What have you been up to again?" she asked.

"Aha! You've been ferreting about while I was away," said Otto and smiled. "Darling, did you think we could have got a room in Schloss Cobenzl after midnight if you hadn't been my wife?"

Roserl was silent.

The night porter returned with a key. "Unfortunately, I've nothing left on the first floor, but on the second I still have a fine room, with a wonderful view over the city."

"Exactly," said Otto, "I thought so. *En avant la musique.*"

A Viennese night porter does not need to know

French, but he must know that the aristocracy likes to speak French. This functionary was satisfied of Otto's distinction by this further evidence, taken in conjunction with his general appearance. As regards the lady, she made a good although not quite correct impression: some dry blades of grass, bits of moss were still clinging to her skirt—but even an aristocratic couple may have a mad prank in the Wienerwald. The night porter was a good-natured man. He took them to their room, accepted without exaggerated gratitude a five-schilling note, and bade them good night.

"Otto," said Roserl, looking round her, "what do you mean by coming to Schloss Cobenzl? It's much, much too expensive."

"Not for just this once, Rosamündchen. I've always had an atavistic feeling that I wanted to carry you off with me to my Schloss: *'er hob das Magdlein im Sattel'*—that's no doubt why I'm so pleased to be on this historic spot with you now."

"Nonsense!" said Roserl, and threw her little hat on the table. "Schloss Cobenzl isn't an historic spot. It's an hotel."

"Count Philipp von Cobenzl, who was the grandfather of my grandmother, built his palace in the middle of this handsome park and passed away in 1810," said Otto as though delivering a lecture. "You can read it in any Baedeker. Come along, my lady wife, let's go and see whether he chose an attractive spot."

Through the balcony doors the balmy night wind was wafted; it was unexpected after the still, summer atmosphere of the Wienerwald. Otto stepped outside and put both his hands on the balustrade. The sky stood, very high and gleaming white with moonlight, above the wooded slopes that ran down to his feet and away to the plain in which lay the city. Vineyards and cornfields formed the transition; they lay in the white moonlight like dark and light squares outspread against the hills. The eye could follow the late pedestrian along their edge. Otto leant over: immediately below him stood the terraces, bordered with red climbing roses. 'These terraces must date from Philipp's time,' he thought, and suddenly felt very proud of their fairy-like beauty. Then he laughed, amused by his own mania for grandeur.

"Come along, Rosamündchen," he called inside, and when Roserl came he placed his arm about her shoulders. "Look, dearest. Here I lay my woods and my fields and all my belongings at your adorable little feet." He made a wide theatrical gesture embracing the horizon, and then unexpectedly kissed his favorite spot in Roserl's neck.

Roserl leaned her head against his arm without saying anything, and Otto carefully laid his cheek against her temple and its wave of silken hair. Softly and fervently he kissed her forehead, enveloped it

251

with tender caresses. But she remained motionless, uttering no word. It was an unknown experience, that she could be so quiet as she was this evening. For years he had carried in his ears the memory of her chattering, girlish voice. But in her quietness she was wholly dear to him—more precious than she had ever been. There was such a motherly indulgence in her being that suddenly he felt all his tendernesses to be boyishly inadequate.

And then he realized that he was no longer sure of her. He had had her in his arms, yes; but afterwards she had withdrawn herself. Now she was herself again, a human being with her own mysteries. Her being had wrapped itself anew in the gentle gravity that attracted and disconcerted him at the same time. But he did not want to feel disconcerted, and so he strained himself to vanquish this gravity, this wise, restful gentleness. He did not want her to be wise. He wanted to hear her laugh, and to laugh with her; he wanted to be gay as in the old days, to be happy for six days—that should be possible—and then he would see.

"Just look, Rosamündchen—they've actually lit up the city for us there below. They've lit up all the little lights along all the streets. Now tell me what you see, little one. What's that half circle over there?"

"That's the Ring." Obediently Roserl followed his pointing finger. "And beyond there's the Praterstern, and here close by, of course, is the Grinzingerstrasse

—and there? That's the moon shining on the Danube. But further along is the Reichsbrücke."

"Quite right," said Otto, "that's not bad for someone Hungarian born. But now tell me, what's that little red light away to the right?"

"The Westbahnhof?" suggested Roserl dubiously.

"No, silly girl, those are the illuminated signs of Korngross's—you really ought to have known that."

"But it can't be. They're enormously large!"

"Yes, but from here they're infinitesimally small; and behind them, right in the depths, lies the Luftbadgasse, which of course you can't see. And that's where we really belong; but now we're standing nicely on the battlements of my Schloss. Laugh, little girl!"

"Otto," said Roserl, apologetically, stroking the hand that lay about her shoulders. "Otto, I can't laugh easily any more. Really. I believe I'm too old, too old for games. I can't join in any more. I see through it all the time, that they're only games. Everybody must give up playing sometime, I think. One a little sooner, another later. Darling, I'm glad I was able to come to you once more. I'm very glad you took me with you this evening; but I can't make a little game of it any longer. I'm too much aware that I'm standing on the battlements of a castle in the air."

"But that's not true," cried Otto, puckering his eyebrows. "You mustn't say that. I know well enough that I was talking a lot of nonsense just now; but when you were lying beside me, that wasn't a little

253

game, that wasn't a castle in the air. That was real, and even though I shan't be here in a few days, it will continue to be real, and nobody can take it away from us."

"No, that's the point. I shall be thinking of it and go on thinking of it, and be even more lonely. Otto——" Roserl had pressed her face to his breast, her two arms embraced him, tightly, more tightly; there was a desperate will in her grasp. "Otto, I can't stay alone any more. You made me into a woman. Now nobody else can mean anything to me. I know that—I've been through everything. When you're gone, I've no future. Do you remember what you said last time? You said: 'I don't want to stand in your way. You must marry and have a husband and children.' Otto, that doesn't exist for me any more. You'll always stand in the way—there's only one man for me, and for him, if need be, I'll give up children. Otto, you must take me away with you. This time you must take me away with you. I can't go on being alone like this."

"I've nothing to offer you," said Otto, and pulled himself upright defensively. From her grasp he felt how anxiously she was waiting for his reply; but obstinately, word by word, all the considerations he had formerly repeated to himself returned to his brain. "I can't take you away. I'm not sure one day that I shall be able to look after you the next. That's how it was, and that's how it still is. You know that, and you also know that you certainly have a future here—at Korngross's."

"You won't understand me," said Roserl, sighing, and she let go of him. "You won't understand me because you're too proud. You think it isn't fair to take me with you, but that's only a word. In reality, it doesn't fit in with your conception of honor to take something from a woman that you can't return. But that's because you don't understand what giving and taking is for a woman, because you're nothing but a big foolish boy who asks what's done and what isn't done. If you leave me here alone, with or without Korngross's, I've no future, I, Rosita Goldös whom you held a little while ago in your arms. The head cashier of Korngross's will certainly be given the power to sign. Oh, you can rest assured of that; but that's not the real woman. You did not kiss her awake when she was twenty. But Rosita must come with you, do you hear? She can't bear Fräulein Goldös's pleasant life, even if she could buy up the whole of Korngross's. You must take her with you. God! I'll cook for you and slave for you and mend your clothes—and it's not altogether impossible that I might get a little job over there; but I won't remain alone again. I can't do that any more."

"And was that why you didn't want to come with me this evening?" said Otto. He had to swallow; there was a strange dryness in his throat. "I'm sorry, Roserl. I really didn't understand that—otherwise

255

perhaps I shouldn't have dared call on you. You're right. We can't play little games any more. Now I must really go away—but tonight we must still stay with one another. There's nothing to be done about that now."

He had spoken softly, almost in a whisper. He felt how she withdrew herself. She took a step sideways towards the balustrade, and he did not venture to look at her. But he knew that he could not do otherwise. 'I must not,' he thought, 'I must not take her with me to be my drudge. I can't let myself be waited on and looked after by a woman I don't wish to marry. And marry her I may not. I'm the last—I may not deny everything all those others before me have upheld. I haven't the right to do that. It's impossible, impossible.' He clung to the word. He pressed it into his consciousness: it was impossible to marry her, and equally impossible to abuse her. It must not be. One must remain conscious of what is and is not done.

'You shouldn't have gone to see her again after all that has happened, and what you said at the time.'

In the most unexpected fashion his conscience was assailed with this mortifying thought, and refused inexorably to be lulled. Yes, it was incomprehensible to him now how he could have run to her in such haste that morning. He had had no such intention. How could he have done it? Disquietened, he gave Roserl a sidelong glance: and then all his reasonable and unreasonable thoughts were washed away by the flood of sympathy that streamed towards her. She stood there, leaning helplessly against the balustrade, her arms hanging limply to her sagging knees. Otto was instantly beside her. He took her against him, and felt her short sob tremble through his own body.

Thus they stood, pressed closely together, two human beings between the wide sky and the far-flung expanse below them. Their tired heads bent towards one another for consolation; but there was no consolation. His hand stroked her hair absently, slowly and more slowly. His fingers felt the soft hair, and the curve of the crown of her head fitted into the rounded palm of his hand. He did not know that he was caressing her head as if she were a little girl. His eyes stared away into the wide, white lit heaven. The lights of the city were only childish dots in the distance; they shimmered under the gleaming silver expanse of heaven. The moonlight was a cool, white, unearthly milk. It dripped from the vine leaves and poured over the climbing roses that held up their wide open pink chalices. A single transparent veil of cloud came drifting by; without weight, it overspread the pale disk of the moon. Then softly it was wafted further on by the summer night wind. Everything was clear and pure and transparent. The whole world lay there still, without will and without haste.

Otto also stood without will and without haste. His hand repeated endlessly its quiet caressing movement over Roserl's hair. His thoughts had wandered far along strange paths; only a vague echo reverberated. 'It's impossible—not possible.' But his hand had a life of its own, experienced the intimacy of the motionless bowed head that surrendered to his caress.

And then the hand reached further, glided over a smooth cheek, and pressed the dear head against a breast that suddenly breathed deep, wonderfully freed and brimming over with joy. Otto felt it with a shock: this was the only possible reality. He was back in himself. His mind was made up. His arms surrounded the girl's slim body.

"God help us! for we can't do otherwise," said he. "Darling, I believe I too could no longer be without you. Could you love me? Ordinarily, if you were with me every day, and saw what I'm like?"

"Yes," said Roserl, and closed her eyes.

"Then we'll have to see that we make you Mrs. Wernizek as soon as possible."

FATHER, can I come in?"

The eldest son had knocked at the bedroom door behind which Father and Mother Hodl were preparing for the night. They had not wanted to admit that they were tired, but in the end they had allowed themselves to be sent to their bedroom when the last guests had departed; the children would clear up the worst of the mess. Now they had nearly finished their toilet for the night: two little gray plaits hung over Resi's stiffly starched nightgown, and Johannes was standing in his vest and pants, which of course he kept on at night—it was a mistake to make life unnecessarily complicated. But Johannes was quite fit to be seen in his snow-white underwear: Resi kept him as fresh and spotless as herself. The old couple really offered a joyful little picture to the son, who entered the room in answer to Hodl's "Come in!"

"I've come to say good night. We've got through the worst, you know. The others have gone. Tomorrow morning I'll come along early to put everything straight again."

"Oh, no," said Hodl, "the workmen can do that. You just sleep a little longer. But perhaps one of your girls will come along to help Grandmother."

"Don't think of it," said Resi decisively. "I prefer to take a little longer over it myself. I want to put everything in place myself. It'll all get straight, my boy—but you go home now too. It's already gone two."

"Yes, I'm going," said Johannes junior, and cleared his throat. "But I've something to tell you. I could have told you tomorrow morning, but perhaps it's better for you to know tonight.—You might have got into some trouble. Tonight a couple of detectives were here—"

"Detectives?" asked Hodl.

"Yes, for that boy of Jonathan's."

"That's nice!" said Hodl. "But it doesn't surprise me. Of course that trouble-maker is the leader of his cronies; monkeys, they are, those student gentry. The old man runs himself off his legs in order to let that boy study, and what does he get for his pains? Dishonor and ingratitude.—But let me catch that gentleman again in my workshop!"

"You won't catch him there for some time. They took him away handcuffed."

"God Almighty!" Shocked, Hodl fell silent. Handcuffed? Then there was something more behind it than a mere students' riot. Anxiously he stared before him with furrowed brow. His world had suddenly turned and presented another, grimmer aspect to him: all the shocking reports that just appeared of an evening in the paper assumed a disquieting shape and reality. He had seen and read those reports year in, year out. The world was changing, and the news that staggered a man today was stale tomorrow: a well-known fact. In the meantime something else, something worse, had happened; but it was and remained only news in the newspaper. A man could not feel absolutely broken about it: there was a great difference between printed news and the real world. If one of the little Bergmanns came home with a gash in its head, that was worse than that the police had apparently shot down several demonstrators in Floridsdorf. The newspaper, after all, came every day in any case with news, and when these had been read —ah, well, then, it was done with. But this, about that Jonathan boy, that was not done with. This had happened, and had consequences, tangible and visible consequences; for the old man upstairs of course, but also for Hodl himself, who would certainly have to be a witness. They would be wondering what had happened and how it had come about, for it had happened here, here in this well-known house. Here, on this small spot of the immeasurable world, a human being had been seized by other human beings, and handcuffs had been clapped round his wrists.

"What's he done?" asked Resi.

"I don't know." The son shrugged his shoulders. "The detectives of course let nothing out; they took him away at once in a taxi."

"He can't be an ordinary thief or murderer,"

261

decided Hodl. He did not want to represent the case to himself as more painful than necessary.

"And in any case, he's not coming back into the house," declared Resi.

"No; here in the house, that won't do," deliberated Hodl. "What does the old man say? Of course you went upstairs at once, Johannes?"

"Look here," said Johannes junior, offended, "there's been no opportunity this evening. You ought to understand that. Besides, what could I have done there? You go yourself tomorrow. Well, you know it now. Good night, both!"

"Come here, boy," said Resi. "We haven't thanked you yet." She drew his head downwards and kissed him with motherly gratitude on both cheeks. "Dear, it was a wonderful day—but now you must be getting home. You'll be feeling your legs."

"Thanks also, Johannes," said Hodl, and pressed the hand of his eldest as man to man. "I hear your boys are already getting busy over your silver wedding. That's what comes of a good example. Bye-bye." He put out his hand in parting; but Mother Resi followed her son through the entrance hall—after all, there was nobody to see her in her nightgown. The great main gate was already closed, but the wicket in the right door was still ajar. The son stepped outside. When he looked round, he saw his mother in the half-darkness only as a white spot. Still, he knew she was standing there waving, so he waved too. He cast a last glance at the façade and walked rapidly away. It had been a busy day, but he was satisfied. He had got through it with honor.

Resi still stood listening a moment to his steps that echoed from the street dully and more dully. Then she closed the wicket; but Johannes had the key and would have to lock up. Yes, now the golden wedding was over. The last feast day allotted to a human being lay behind her. It gave her a feeling of emptiness. There was nothing to look forward to—except the last sacrament. Then it would all be over. Resi shook her head slowly, then groped her way back through the unlit entrance hall, relying upon the light that came from her own room. It was almost unbelievable that a moment ago this place had been so boisterous and crowded. The stillness was the more oppressive. Her foot caught in a rustling paper streamer. She stumbled, and was on the point of crying. Himmel!—she would not cry. Tomorrow she must be fit in order to clear up the dirty mess.

When she entered the bedroom, she ran to Johannes.

"What's up now?" she asked, for Johannes was standing once more in his trousers and his black cloth coat that she had already hung in its folds over a chair.

"I'm just going to see after the lights," said Johannes. "The boys did say they'd done it, but I only half trust anyone else."

Resi nodded. It was indeed an important thing

263

that the gas jets on the staircase should be properly turned off at nights. "You might at the same time close the wicket," said she.

And so Johannes went and did his round, as his father and grandfather had done before him—each in his own way. The one blew out oil lamps and candles, the other turned down paraffin wicks. His own son later on would turn off switches, but Johannes was quite satisfied with his gas, and his lodgers had to be so too. Besides which, if necessary, he could have found his way through the house in the dark— he knew the feel of every stair under his feet. He still lived in the house he owned: he was not a skinflint, as the seditious riff-raff would have liked to call after him. When in the evenings, he went through the steps and passages of his house in the stillness of the night, he felt responsible for all those sleeping, breathing human beings who were at rest under his roof.

On the second floor he put his ear to Herr Bergmann's front door. Everything there was peaceful; even the newly born infant seemed to be sleeping with the others. Hodl remained quite a minute bent to the keyhole. Then, with a smile, he went on.

The sons really had conscientiously turned off all the gas taps. He looked up to the third floor: that landing was in darkness too. And then he seized the banisters after all, and without stumbling went up the stairs on tiptoe.

Exactly; he had expected that. Through the crack

at the threshold of Meyer Jonathan's flat came a strip of light: the old man was still up. Hodl's hand reached out towards the bell, and then it fell again; he stood on the dark landing peering at the chink of light. He strained his hearing to catch a sound, but everything was quiet in the flat.

Again he stretched out his hand, and again it sank away hesitatingly.

Hodl was a man of the lower middle class. He was not tainted with the fear of the over-civilized, who shudder so deeply at contact with human grief that they keep themselves fastidiously at a distance from those who are in trouble. Hodl was without this fear. He himself had had to bear grief, and knew by experience how consoling the pressure of a fellow human being's hand can be. He would have liked to stand by Meyer Jonathan in his heavy hour. But would Herr Jonathan want to receive him?

Also, of course, landlord Hodl had a certain right to know what went on under his roof, and it was this right that finally gave him courage to pull the bell.

Two seconds later, Meyer Jonathan opened the door wide. He stood, very erect and very grave, upon the threshold; but when he saw who the visitor was, he beckoned him in in friendly fashion.

"I saw you still had a light on—that's why I rang," began Hodl, and broke off searching for further words. Suddenly he was completely disconcerted. He could not understand this: if one of his many grandsons had been fetched by the police, he would have crept into a corner with misery and shame; and here opposite him stood the little Jew who had seen his sole grandson carried away to prison, and yet looked at him with eyes as clear and open as ever, even directed him to a chair, as if he had come to pay an expected and pleasant visit.

But Hodl did not sit down. Hastily and ill at ease, he sought within himself for something to say, all the more restlessly because Meyer Jonathan stood waiting there so quietly. When he could no longer endure his own uncertainty, he began afresh: "I haven't locked up downstairs yet, Herr Jonathan—and I thought—perhaps your grandson has the key of the house—and if you want to go out tonight for one thing or another. . . ." He heard himself stammer; this was not what he had wanted to say. But then who could have approached this venerable old man with unbidden consolation?

When he gave it up at last, and stood there with a a flushed face, Meyer nodded to him understandingly. "Thank you very much, Herr Hodl. It's very friendly of you to come along and see. Yes, a great misfortune has befallen us. So you've heard of it already; but I won't trouble you with it this evening. It's not necessary. There's nothing that needs haste—nothing. It can wait till tomorrow. You just go quietly to bed, Herr Hodl. You must be tired after your feast-day. Good night—and thank you very much."

Then Hodl had to go. Meyer Jonathan waited in the lighted rectangle of the door until the steps of the staircase ceased to creak. Then he closed the door noiselessly and returned to his room. There he resumed the place where he had stood in prayer, his face turned towards the East. What did a night without sleep matter to old Meyer Jonathan, who all his life had been accustomed to spend the nights of fast days awake and praying? Could he not watch and pray for one night for the son of his son? And he was not unworthy, he for whom he wished to be the intercessor before God. When he had asked: "What have you done, boy?" Daniel had answered: "Nothing of which I need be ashamed."

Downstairs Hodl sat on the side of his bed and slowly slipped off his socks. Everything was shut, all the lights were extinguished. The day was over, a great day with few disappointments. He was contented, very contented and thankful that the day had been as it had been. He was filled with contentment; and now that he was preparing for the coming sleep he was also tired, very, very tired. He did not protest against this tiredness, he was quite prepared to feel to the very limit how tired he was: when a man was getting old, he had a right to be tired after a long day. He did not mind, either, feeling how his knees were shaking. Yes, there was an end to everything: there had been a time when his knees could not have shaken as they did now.

Resi was standing before the great cupboard, putting away her gold chain in one of its many mysterious little drawers. Each time she buried her trinkets in another corner of the old piece of furniture. Johannes looked on smiling—women never grew wise. Then Resi laid out a pile of dusters for the next morning, and a clean smock for Johannes who would have to begin again. Johannes watched. Absentmindedly, he stared at the smoothly ironed painter's smock. Yes, tomorrow of course he would get going again—how much longer?

It was not an anxious question, this "how much longer?" There was a time for coming and a time for going. It had always been so. He had seen it when he was a young man and his grandfather had had to hand over the work to his father. After that, his father had gone, and in his turn handed over the work to his son. Now the time was coming when he himself would have to hand over the work. It might be a little shorter or a little longer, but he knew he was already many years on the way he must go. Ah, well, the work remained; there would always be painting in the world. At the moment, times were bad, but there had often been bad times since the Hodls began, and the business still endured. For good work, people would always need a Hodl.

Johannes slowly smoothed a sock over his knee. A

great thought was engrossing him. If there was always work for everybody, work that had to be done and done well, the world would look a different place.

Then he shrugged his shoulders: a man must not think as far as that. The world was too big—it could not be envisaged. But he was grateful that in his own small world he had been able to do his work and keep his good name.

The socks were hanging over the bedrail. "Haven't you finished yet, Resi?" asked Johannes. "Do hurry up, woman." And lightly—because women after all understood nothing of the great, simple things that matter—he said with an air of innocence: "I've just been sitting thinking, woman: Johannes is already forty-eight. I must begin to think of handing everything over to him and his boys."